Korean Odyssey

Korean Odyssey

Martin Samuel

PARTRIDGE

A Penguin Random House Company

To order additional copies of this book, contact
Toll Free 800 101 2657 (Singapore)
Toll Free 1 800 81 7340 (Malaysia)
orders.singapore@partridgepublishing.com

www.partridgepublishing.com/singapore

"Snakes!" she screamed. "Help me Minsu, I'm falling; don't let me fall!" begged the young girl. Frantically, the young boy rushed over to where his little sister was and in a frenzied, desperate, attempt quickly laid prone on the damp, leaf littered ground and reached over the top of the hillside as far as he could to where she dangled only a few meters above a pit full of venomous mamushi vipers. With no fear that he might fall himself, he reached down and gripped on to the hood of her jacket and pulled and pulled as hard as he could with every bit of strength he had hoping he would be strong enough to save his little sister from such a horrible fate. The thought of losing Jimin after the grief and sadness of Oonky added to his determination, and fueled his will to save his little sister. The deadly, hemorrhagic toxins from the bites of the vipers' razor sharp teeth would have brought a slow and painful death to the young girl causing severe internal bleeding and eventually shutting down her life support functions. Horror and fear flashed through the young girl's mind like a nightmare as the terror that loomed below was real and waiting. The fear and agony of the fall and the deadly painful end all sent a shrill of terror down her spine. Looking down into the pit at the revulsion of them writhing and squirming, interlaced in a kaleidoscopic collage of brown, grey and olive colors with their hideous, long, thin garden hose shapes, all hissing and coiled among the rocks in a shallow pit just below her feet added to the little girl's panic and fear. As Minsu desperately reached down farther and farther to get a better position to exert his maximum strength, Jimin's frantically kicking feet clamored for a ledge or root or anything that could provide a means of escape up the soft brown cliff of crumbling earth, roots and leaves.

In the small South Korean city of Sacheon nestled on the southern coast in Gyeongsangnamdo province, it was a beautiful, warm, spring day without a cloud in the sky. The sun was shining, the birds were singing and the welcoming new sights of spring and the day to day sounds of life seemed to fill the air with a feeling of hope and happiness. The children felt a new and welcome recovery to the rain, gloom and lightning of a damp and grim winter that seemed to suddenly end a few days ago as if somebody had just turned off a light switch. Following a visit to the Buddhist monk, earlier in the morning, at the very top of the hill where the concrete road ends both children were overflowing with happiness and brimming with good thoughts and a feeling of relief, which helped to put their unsettled consciences at ease. Oonky, their dearly beloved cat of 15 years (who was older than both of them) died two days ago without any warning or signs of a disease or sickness or anything to indicate a coming death. They needed to talk to someone whom they thought would be able to deal with their grief and sadness. Someone who might have some connection with the afterlife and someone who could let Oonky know how sad and lonely they were without him. Both children remembered the trips to the Buddhist monk with both parents after the devastating loss, three years ago of their older sister Bo-young, when she was killed walking home from school by a large truck. The kind old monk was thrilled to see the children and offered some guidance and hope to deal with the sadness and reassured them that Oonky is always with them in their minds and hearts. With open hands and loving prayers for having not been there when Oonky had passed away both children felt comforted knowing that everything would be all right; the monk assured them that he was safely on his way to a better place.

Anytime they needed to talk about their loss or any other problems, they were always welcome which gave them some confidence and hope that they could visit again.

As the children were walking down the long, white, twisty concrete road flanked with tall dark green Douglas fir trees on either side a loud whining sound seemed to permeate the wide open Sacheon basin. A Korean air force F-50 Golden Eagle trainer was doing "touch and goes" - landings and takeoffs-at the nearby air force base. The excitement and thrill caused Minsu and Jimin to scramble for a clearing on the hillside to get a better look. Running through the wooded area to an opening and standing at the cliff's edge both children stared in wonder and amazement and marveled at the skill with which the pilot controlled the aircraft as it climbed high up and up into the sky, almost out of sight and then would suddenly appear out of nowhere, someplace else at a lightning fast speed not far above where they were standing with the loud whooshing sound from the engine preceding it. The glistening, long thin white object dazzled in the morning sun. Their father Mr. Kim Jeung Ho served as a wing commander in the Korean Air Force during the late 2000s. Many times he would take the children, both of whom were very young at the time, out on day trips to the base to admire the aircraft and meet some of the pilots.

Covered in rotting leaves and dark earthy looking material, certain areas of the cliff, where the children were standing, gave a false and misleading appearance. The mild, wet winter had caused some points on the hillside to experience heavy water run-off with a cascading, waterfall effect down the front of the hillside washing away a lot of earth and stone; over time this led to erosion causing a softening and weakening of the ground. The rainfall had revealed areas such as roots and branches that had long since been buried to be uncovered which on first glance may have appeared to have been firm and strong enough to support an object above it but this was a false and misleading impression.

A lot of the hillside wildlife, due to the rainfall, like earthworms, mice and snakes had to escape their flooded habitats and seek drier ground. The point where Jimin stood was one of those areas composed mostly of exposed roots and branches with nothing of any substance to give it strength like rock or clay to support anything above it. Moving around and shuffling for a better view weakened the ground even more and worse was she didn't pay any attention to the area that she finally chose to position herself on, which only ensured the young girl's fate. Minsu, however, standing farther back on the cliff and just to the right of Jimin was lucky to find a firmer area of larger impacted rocks which appeared to be "cemented" by the dirt around them. All of a sudden, as if walking on thin ice, without any warning the little bit of ground and stone that was left crumbled and fell away like a house of cards and young Jimin found herself dangling just below the top of the hillside. Fortunately for her, in a last second reach with both hands extended she was able to grab on to an exposed tree root and save herself from the deadly consequence that lay below. From there she hanged at an angle "glued" right up against the hillside hanging on for her life hoping that the root wouldn't break and more important that her older brother Minsu would be strong enough to save her. "Keep pulling; pull as hard as you can Minsu! Don't let me fall down there!!" repeated Jimin as Minsu tried with every last bit of power and strength to save his little sister from a horrible and painful death. Staring down at the sight of horror Jimin knew that her life would be over if the root or Minsu failed. "Hang on Jimin, I will save you! See if you can climb up the side! Try to dig your feet into the side; try to stand on a ledge or something." Minsu blurted in a last moment cry of panic and desperation. Grabbing on and holding her hood and pulling as hard as he could he was frustrated by how he could feel his grip gradually loosen no matter how hard, it seemed, he pulled.

Within a short time of what had started out as a peaceful and satisfying trip to the Buddhist monk quickly turned into a struggle between life and death as the tender, young little girl desperately hanged on for her life. With both hands still desperately clinging to the exposed tree root Jimin could not help but look down again and again at the orgy of horror and revulsion. As the 8 year old girl begged for her life she hoped and prayed that her older brother Minsu would be strong enough to get her out of this horrific dilemma.

Desperately struggling, Jimin was in a frantic fight against nature with the omnipotent force of gravity continually adding to the desperate situation. "Pull harder and harder Minsu!! Help me Minsu" was the desperate plea of help as she clung for her life. The constant stream of adrenalin made her grab even firmer to the root. Like most little girls, and some little boys, the thought of those snakes did indeed fill her with a deathly gloom and fear. As the little Jimin squirmed and screamed, with mind numbing shrills Minsu's furiously beating heart gave the young boy a final burst of strength like an Olympic weight lifter at his maximum display giving everything he had to make his final effort; his last shot at victory. In a final burst of power with an almost super human strength which even surprised him by the sudden explosion of energy from his already tired and exhausted muscles, Minsu managed to drag his little sister up from the close perils;

above the jaws of death and over the lip of the edge to the safety of the damp dark brown, leaf littered, flat ground. Once on top both children laid flat on the moist ground exhausted and tired; Jimin was just happy to be out of that terrible situation and saved from certain death. Then the realization of what had happened set in as the little girl began to cry which started out as a whimper and then slowly elapsed into a full outburst of screaming and shrieking with tears streaming down her face. Minsu thought it would be better to just let her cry for as long as she wanted; He was too tired and exhausted to get up and comfort her. He noticed that loose earth had collected on her face which had left dark brown patches on her cheeks and some areas around her eyes and mouth settling on the moist areas of her face after she had more than once brushed up against the exposed areas of the hillside. After a few minutes Minsu put his arm around his little sister and did what he could to try comfort her by whispering in her ear, "Don't cry, everything is all right now… you're OK, you're safe and soon we'll be home," Minsu was just as exhausted and tired and "soothing, soft talk" was all he could really offer; no more than a few soft expressions to stop the torrent of grief and horror that flooded from Jimin. The sound of the valley was quiet and both children were lying on the ground basking in the morning sun after the horrific experience. Minsu found some comfort in the sounds of the birds and trees and for the moment that would be enough to relax him and for the time it would take, he hoped, for Jimin to stop crying. He could not help but wonder at how everything seemed all right and then how the shock after a near death encounter left them both drawn and exhausted. After a short time of lying there Minsu started to feel the cold from the ground and decided to stand up; Jimin, quiet now, glanced up briefly at her older brother, her eyes still full of tears and face covered in brown patches of earth. "Are you all right now? Shall we go?" he asked her in a soft, comforting voice with no sense of hurry. Jimin stared up at him with a look on her face of puzzlement like she had just awakened from a deep sleep, still groggy and dazed and occupied with other thoughts, reeling from the horror of what had happened and not quite able to forget what could have happened. Minsu offered her a hand and after a few moments she reached up and held on to it. As they stood up they could feel the weight of the mud on their clothes and the dampness which made it difficult to move with the thick heavy soil hardening in some places. Minsu's trousers, from the his stomach down were unrecognizable and "caked" with the dark thick brown clay; Jimin's whole back from head to toe and down her right side were completely covered in mud, so thick was it that the clothes she was wearing were indistinguishable-the color and texture completely hidden by the thick brown clay cover. Both children tried to brush each other off but because it was still damp only small "chunks" could be scrapped off leaving their clothing saturated in damp mud. "Let's get out of here", Minsu said to Jimin and in no time the children walked back over the short distance of muddy leaf littered dark brown, uneven ground to the concrete road that cut through the dense green forest like a thin white line streaking through an emerald green mat. "Minsu, I never want to do that again, those snakes were horrible, smelly and ugly", she said still reeling from the trauma of her brush with death. Minsu, walking next to her, staring down at the narrow lateral grooves in the concrete road glanced up at his sister and replied reassuringly in a soft tone of voice, "Yeah, that's for sure, never again for both of us. I was just as scared as you were Jimin but at least we're safe now... The hillside is definitely not safe in some areas."

Back at the site and apart from making a small topographical change to the Sacheon hillside and burying a few snakes, something far more mysterious in terms of modern physics or to be found in any logical or scientific explanation was happening; an event that could only happen in a fantasy story, not the tiny little town of Sacheon. Deep inside the hill with the entrance to the cryptic tomb now exposed aided by Jimin's "landside" a change was occurring that would see unexplainable events in the children's lives. A small icon of Korea's folklore and history would change the lives of the children forever; an ancient warrior of the old Gaya Confederacy imprisoned in an ancient tomb while defending his post on the outskirts of the ancient city of Jinju against the nearby Silla Kingdom warriors was beginning to awaken. After being pursued by a platoon of heavily armed soldiers and cavalry for over two weeks and escaping to the tiny little town of Sacheon, over 1,500 years ago Nam Jae Hoon managed to hide from his pursuers by crawling into a small narrow cave and covering himself in a "box" like tomb secured by a big heavy slab of stone evading any detection. Imprisoned for centuries in a cocoon that nourished and maintained his body by the ancient spirit of Jumeau was an icon from the early Korean days when folklore and tradition ruled the peninsula during the time of the three kingdoms; his life was not finished but put on-hold for a later mission. The sword that he kept and used to defend himself and the Gaya confederacy from many soldiers now had to be put in its rightful place; to be returned to the mighty warrior who was from this area after it was annexed by the Silla kingdom (one of the three in Korea at that time) in AD 562: General Kim Yushin a descendant of the last king of Gaya. Only Ms. Ok Eun Suk matriarch of the Turquoise Palace of Korea Past and Present could accept the sword and put it in its proper place.

But for now, the only thing the children wanted to do was to get home and change out of their dirty, earth laden clothes; a warm shower and something to eat.

Arriving at the back entrance both children were greeted by 2 curious and startled parents the moment they tried to quietly and discretely open the back door to the kitchen. Kim Jeung Ho and Kim Sun Sin were both shocked at their children's appearance and mortified by the account of Jimin's near death experience and the struggle that she endured to avoid an excruciatingly, painful death. Standing in the dim light between the kitchen sink and the refrigerator under the towering height of Mr. Kim and his lovely wife, known to her friends as Miss Korea, both children looked up forlornly and awaited their parent's reprimand. Jimin's little angelic face was still bearing the dirty brown "mask" from the day's big event. After a furious tirade and lecture Mr. Kim mandated in a loud commanding voice, "In future you will stay on the concrete road and not go off into the hillside and that is final! These hills are dangerous and full of snakes and wolves and child molesters so no more hiking on your own! In future we will all go and see the monks at the top of the hill and say our prayers for Oonky together; just ask and we can all go. Now go upstairs and get cleaned and put on your pajamas. Tonight for dinner we are having Kim chi, Bulgogi and some ice cream."

Both children glanced at each other, sighed and then turned to go to the bathroom at the top of the stairs; since Jimin was the one most in need she was the first to go; Minsu waited in the garage because he was covered in too much dirt to sit on his bed or wait in the kitchen.

After dinner and too tired for television or even the thought of homework both Minsu and Jimin went to their own bedrooms, got into bed and quickly fell asleep. It was still quite early, not even 6 pm but for both of them it had been a long and exhausting day and one that would stay in their minds for the rest of their lives.

As the children slept and dreamed of happier times change was still at the scene of where it all began; deep inside the Sacheon hill what happened the day before and the "awakening" was in its final phase.

Slowly sliding back the top of the sarcophagus and exposed by a dark green, almost luminescent light which nourished and sustained him for hundreds of years Nam Jae Hoon began to get up. Climbing out of the tomb and thrusting open the door that lead to the tomb emerging in the bright sun light looking down at the terrain in front of him and then stepping over some snakes: some dead, some alive and some still in shock this specimen from a distant, almost forgotten past was both curious and amused; not at all shocked and stunned by the new sights, sounds and smells of a modern day Korea. Standing at just less than 2 meters tall and wearing a tall Korean military helmet with typical military dress from the period Nam Jae Hoon panned the horizon until his vision came to rest on Dongseong Elementary school to the scene of where his two rescuers were located. Flexing his arms and stretching every muscle in his body after a very long sleep Nam Jae Hoon made his way quickly and purposefully over the rice fields that were at this time laying fallow as he walked over the rows of hoed ground and then onto the highway that led to Jinju from Sacheon. At the time of Nam Jae Hoon's imminent arrival the school yard was full of children running around and playing football; it was lunch time and even though Nam Jae Hoon thought about walking up to the cafeteria and helping himself to some delicious Doengsong School khimche he was afraid that his appearance might cause some panic, chaos and terrify the unsuspecting school children and teachers. Lying in wait on the other side of the service road and between the irrigation canals, vigilant of any passers-by that might see him Nam Jae Hoon waited in silence. He needed a special strategy to present himself as the benevolent and caring being he was but was wary about how to do it; his appearance might shock and scare the children away. He was so grateful to Minsu and Jimin for releasing him from his many centuries long imprisonment but needed their help to return the sword. He thought that it would be better if he stayed hidden where he was and waited for the school to finish. He could present himself to the children as they went home since they lived behind the school and would therefore have to walk up the service road.

At four o'clock the bell rang and the children gathered up their belongings and flooded out the front and back entrances in a stampede all anxious to get home. Minsu and Jimin were in different parts of the school so whoever was first waited by the back doors for the other one to come. Minsu, being in a higher grade level, was usually waiting for Jimin since the higher grade levels were closer to the ground floor; Jimin took a little longer being smaller and less able than her bigger brother to move as quickly. Minsu waited by the door and saw Jimin eventually come down the stairs in what looked like a rush with hundreds of other children all hurrying, pushing and shoving to get to the front and rear doors. As Jimin got closer to where he was waiting, Minsu stared and was startled by what he thought were some of the dark brown dirt marks from what had happened the day before when her face bore the dirt splotches. As she got closer to where he was standing they seemed to fade away; dull lighting and his own vivid memory, he thought to himself.

The children walked hand in hand out the rear gate with the throngs of other children all rushing to get home and all trying to get across the main road. They managed to walk over the short bridge that traversed the irrigation canal to the narrow service road. Occasionally one would see a "rice harvester": a vehicle with a small engine sitting on a two wheeled separate framework two meters in front of the driver and controlled by a long steering mechanism much like the handlebars and elongated forks on a custom "chopper" motorcycle. As the children walked along the three-and-a half-meter wide concrete road they noticed a rice harvester coming towards them. From a distance it looked like any other rice harvester and appeared quite normal but as the vehicle approached things started to appear not so ordinary. Minsu told Jimin to watch the vehicle as it got closer but Jimin was already looking at it and like her brother was trying to figure out what on earth the driver was wearing on his head. Anybody that might have seen it might have wondered the same thing. As the vehicle drew closer questions began to arise like what on earth was that bright shiny object that the driver was wearing over his chest? It looked like some sort of a breast plate, an ancient military plaque of armor from many bygone days; a past that Korea hasn't seen for a long, long time. As the vehicle drew closer and closer, the children could see a tall pointy conical shape covered by a light brown burlap sack. No rice farmer or anybody that they had ever seen ever wore clothes like that and as the vehicle got right next to the children barely two meters away the driver turned off the engine and asked the children if they missed Oonky. "Oonky", replied Minsu with a curious intonation. "How do you know about Oonky?" asked Jimin just as curious and confused as Minsu. "I know that yesterday Jimin almost died from a fall into a pit of deadly snakes. I was there and helped Jimin avoid a terrible accident," replied Nam Jae Hoon in a gentle, calming tone. "We didn't see you anywhere." replied Minsu. "I was there Minsu and just as terrified at what could have happened to Jimin. Do you remember that sudden burst of strength that you had-the one that really saved Jimin's life?" replied Nam Jae Hoon feeling that he had gained a little of the children's confidence. "If it hadn't been for my contribution you would have lost your little sister forever." "Yes, I remember I gained some extra strength that almost lifted me off the ground! That was from you?" replied

Minsu in a curious tone. "How do you know our names anyway?" retorted Jimin in a pejorative tone. "I know your names from when you were calling each other. I know lots of things" Nam Jae Hoon replied in the same soothing manner and looking at the children with a smile trying to ease the strain of the situation. He then introduced himself to the curious inquisitive children, "My name is Nam Jae Hoon and your close death encounter Jimin released me from a long confinement; you opened a porthole and awakened me from a deep sleep and for that I am eternally grateful to both of you. I have been waiting and waiting for a very long time to get my life back and continue with my future plans, but I need your help." The children looked at each other and then back at Nam Jae Hoon, "What can we do for you? As you can see we are both still very young and not really able to do much. After what happened yesterday it will be very difficult for us to get away since we live at home. Our mom and dad were both very angry at what happened to Jimin and told us that we can't go into the Sacheon hills again without their permission or knowledge." Minsu informed him in a pleading manner. It was getting late and the children told Nam Jae Hoon that they had to get home otherwise there would be consequences to be paid. He understood their situation so he stood up and got out of the vehicle and as he stood up both children gasped in amazement at the size of the ancient Gaya warrior. The children stood in front and looked up at him in much the same way a person would marvel at a very tall building; looking first at the base and then slowly panning up to the top with their focus resting on his tall brown conical shaped helmet and the bright red ribbon that hung from it. Jimin could feel a certain terror; scared as he stood on the service road in full view; she tried to turn and run away but her older brother held her hand tightly at his side with sharp downward thrusts making sure she didn't leave. His stature and appearance made him look like a super hero with the iron and leather armor shining in the late afternoon sun. Unknown to Minsu and Jimin was the fact that now since he had made contact with them only they could see him. The fact that he had been lying in a suspended form of animation in a "tomb" under a hill of dirt and dampness for the last 1,550 years remarkably showed no signs of wear, corrosion or age. Still wearing his ancient armor and looking every bit the warrior he was as the great defender of the failed Gaya Confederacy he reached down and offered a hand to the children. With a certain apprehension and hesitancy Minsu reached up and grabbed the polar bear sized "mitt" of a hand with his hand and with that both children instantly felt a sense of warmth, comfort and safety in the presence of the giant being.

Then in what seemed like the flash of a light or the burst of a firework the children and Nam Jae Hoon were instantaneously elevated to a different place and time thousands of meters above a different Korea. Sequestered by a transparent, membranous, sheath much like an embryo is protected by a sack inside a mother's womb all three beings, with the exception really of one that was debatable as to exactly what he was, defied modern physics or any aeronautical equation of lift and thrust as they looked down on a Korea that showed major historical events in a three dimensional aspect; each historical episode was like an icon as it was happening as they moved over the territory or geographical location of where it happened right below and easily viewed from the vantage point and comfort of their "vehicle." The children sat on either side of Nam Jae Hoon much like they were sitting on a living room sofa as their vehicle of fantasy and dream moved high above the Korean landscape in a nature defying state. The children could see the remarkable maneuvers of Yi Sun Sin as they were happening and his brilliant naval tactics with the "turtle boats" that happened hundreds of years ago as he helped to defeat the invading Japanese during the Imjin War; another area showed the very invention of the Hangul alphabet with King Sejong the Great, the fourth King of the Joseon Dynasty sitting with his scribes. And then in an instant it was all over; the children were standing next to Nam Jae Hoon in the same location where it all began. Remarkably no time had passed since they were first elevated to their out-of-this world adventure. Nam Jae Hoon had taken them through a porthole into another "dimension" where time had no meaning. The children were dazed and amazed at what had just happened, so happy and grateful to their new friend for the brief adventure he had given them. "Well children", he asked "Did you enjoy yourselves?" "Yes we did." replied Minsu with the excitement of a young child who had just been given every present for Christmas. When can we do that again!?" asked Minsu in a thrilled and eager manner wanting to go back on what seemed like the most exciting amusement park ride ever. "That was great Mr. Nam Jae Hoon and thank you so much." Jimin exclaimed with the same joy and enthusiasm as Minsu, having just experienced the most thrilling and wonderful adventure of her life.

As the children were still "glowing" from their out-of the-world experience Nam Jae Hoon reached down and removed two small semi-circular objects about the size of a small saucer; a bright golden object from his scabbard and presented it to the children. The children looked at them and saw that they had the Ying and Yang shape of the modern Korean flag; they both fit together like two pieces in a jigsaw puzzle. "Listen to me carefully children. At the base of Jinju Castle in the Southwest corner you will find a round support pillar which is different from the others. Take these two piece gold amulets that interlock and hold them together; wave it over the base pillar once and you will pass through the "entrance" that will take you back to my time where my brother Nam Jae Young awaits. Once you go through you will find yourself in the same location as when you left but long before the castle was ever built. Reaching down into his sheath that rested on his left side he withdrew his mighty sword holding it up vertically with the tip pointing to the sky. The weapon glistened and sparkled in the setting sun as he handed the sword to Minsu placing the handgrip in Minsu's hand. "I want you to present this sword to Ms. OK Eun Suk who is the matriarch of the Turquoise Palace of Past and Present in Gunju of Siljik province. You are the "master of the sword and I am depending on you to give it to Ms. OK Eun Suk." Nam Jae Hoon towered well above the children talking to them in much the same way a parent would instruct on a matter of great importance as they attentively stood back and looked up to him. "Why can't you come with us?" retorted Minsu in a submissive, contrite manner. "I can't go back as it is not possible for me to travel back to that period. I have been defending my city of Jinju from the looting Silla settlement's soldiers by constantly raiding and antagonizing them using guerilla tactics in an effort to repel the invasion of their pillaging forces. I have been hiding from their deadly search and destroy missions for a long, long time buried under an earthen mound; many of my people had been killed by their rape and destroy tactics. My kingdom lost the battle to remain independent a long time ago and now I give up the lost struggle; conceding this sword is my indication of surrender. After the sword is given to Ms OK Eun Suk I will be able to rest and pass on from this life. "How will we get back to this time?" Minsu asked inquiring in his high pitched voice. In order to return to the future, after you concede the sword to Ms. Ok Eun Suk, hold the two pieces together and say, "We miss Sacheon." Nam Jae Hoon said in a calming, relaxing tone. "Will we be safe?" asked Minsu in a curious tone. "Stay together and follow the directions of my brother and no harm will come to you; he can't protect me but he will be able to protect you" replied Nam Jae Hoon. "What about our parents and the worry they will have if we are gone for a long time?" asked Jimin in a troubled and confused manner. "Your parents won't know you have gone; time has no meaning where you are going so they won't notice anything." he replied in a soothing, comforting, manner. "We should be going home now." said Minsu in an urgent "let's go" manner. "Tomorrow after school we will do as you wish." Minsu assured Nam Jae Hoon. Both children looked at each other and then turned to continue their walk home when Nam Jae Hoon in a last second forgot-to-tell burst of information told the children in a rewarding tone, "For your efforts you will be rewarded with greater mental riches and power. After you pass through the door you will greet my brother Nam Jae Young and he will direct you to meet the beautiful matriarch of the Turquoise Place Ms. OK Eun Suk. My brother will assist you on your journey and you will present this sword to Ms OK Eun Suk." At this point the children were excited and eager to start their trek to the other world and also eager to get home since it was late and they were hungry. After dinner and an hour of homework both children retired to their own bedrooms where they laid in thought and reflected on the day's events. Next morning they were excited and a little anxious about their new task. The first class in the morning-English class-something that Minsu had dreaded saw a change come over the boy as he began to notice a subtle difference in his approach and manner to the task ahead of him. As Ms. Ha Ji Wan handed out the English grammar work sheets the boy could suddenly feel a boost in his confidence. The source may have been elusive or hard to pinpoint but Minsu was certainly feeling more confident in his ability to match the verb with the subject pronoun worksheet. Before he panicked, with anxiety and fear getting the upper hand but now he could feel a change; a gradual transformation in his ability to deal with basic spelling and grammar had become easier; a boost in confidence imbued the boy. After solving some spelling problems correctly and using the words in sentences there was an undeniable increase of self confidence and a sense of can do anything and with more problems successfully solved Minsu actually started to enjoy the class and even felt a sense of accomplishment. Likewise, his little sister two floors above had always struggled with English grammar and basic letter formation but after coming up to the front of the class, her teacher Eeenamin could sense a change in the young girl just by the way she approached the board. Before she would come up with the look of a child about to be punished for violating some classroom rule but for the first time Eenamin was surprised by the look and countenance of an "almost different person" just by how she took the board marker from her hand and how she began to write on the green board. Ms. Elly, as she was better known by her English name, noticed the change as if she were looking at a different child when Jimin wrote a sentence on the board using the correct article of "a" or "an". Jimin finished it with no hesitation standing facing the class confidently holding the marker in her hand offering it back to Ms. Elly with an air of poise and control; indeed she looked like another student. After forming the letter Ms. Elly praised her for her brilliant effort and gave her a pat on the back-a huge long awaited boost of confidence came over the young girl as she returned to her seat, triumphant and "glowing" after her exhibit. Jimin always remembered the encouraging and thoughtful words of her kind and patient Kindergarten teacher Nahdee and the praise and love she had for all of her students and the particular fondness for Jimin. She knew Jimin was a good student and with a little confidence and encouragement her academic skills would illustrate it. Jimin's performance and attitude throughout the rest of the day continued with the same manner and approach of "I can do anything now."

After the bell rang and the school day ended the children gathered up their possessions and made a mad rush for the exits. Minsu always arrived before his sister and like any other day waited near the exit for her to come down the stairs. Today was the day that would probably see one of the biggest events of their lives. Both children were excited and a little anxious about their new endeavor into something that they had absolutely no idea about. Nothing could have prepared them for this journey into a place that was nothing like modern Korea. Once they were both a safe distance away from the school Minsu would give Jimin the other half of the amulet. The bus route was all planned and well reviewed as to how they would get to their destination at Jinju castle. They would walk to the top of the main road near the Korean "pagoda" and catch bus 97; once they got to the Sacheon air force base they would catch bus number 111 which would take them to their final destination and let them off across the road from Jinju castle. Since the two pieces of the amulet interlocked and each of them held the halves that was the assurance that neither one of them would be left behind as they embarked on their bold new adventure of the type that had never ever been done before.

Getting off the bus, crossing the road and arriving at the base of the castle, the children followed Nam Jae Hoon's instructions and made their way to the support pillar at the southwest corner of the castle. As Minsu waved both the amulet halves over the pillar they looked at each other, grabbed each other's hands and then after taking a deep breath, were instantly transferred like a flash of light to a different period a long, long time ago.

In the wink of an eye the children were standing in the same location separated only by lots of days. Suddenly a voice blurted out with a great urgency "Hide, quickly over here!" without any warning or sign the children found themselves with the help of a guiding hand helping them to eschew any detection in the middle of a village being plundered by a cavalry of horsemen screaming and yelling as they raided the community leaving everything to waste in their paths. The children took cover behind the door of a small wooden hut with the help of one very terrified villager. Minsu and Jimin could both smell smoke and were in shock at how quickly things could change; a dense fog from burning wood and grass filled the area. The cavalry men were waving large fire lit sticks and destroying everything in their paths. Most of the wooden huts in the village were either on fire or had been decimated. Scared villagers were seeking cover in the sanctity of any building or structure, even behind a tree or cart, anything that would hide them from the wrath of the heavily clad looting horseback warriors; anything that would provide cover; others watched in terror as whatever they had was destroyed by the ruthless band of warriors. Minsu and Jimin watched in amazement and fright from their vantage point through a hole in the door at the horror of what was happening, not believing what they were seeing; history as it happened so many years ago. They had never experienced anything like this before and were both terrified. Anybody left out in the open at the mercy of the cavalry unit was cut down by a lightning fast sword usually to the neck or the chest. Jimin watched in disgust and horror at how quickly a human head could be severed from the thorax with the lightning fast swoop of a sword. Men, women, children, cattle or anything left in the open all fell victims to the ruthless pillaging whims of the marauding raiders. And then as quickly as it came it was all over. As the soldiers retreated the thundering, terrifying sounds from the horse hoofs with the screams and yells from the horsemen grew quieter and quieter. Slowly life began to emerge and everybody came out from hiding like mice after the cat had gone. Village life returned and the villagers continued with their usual day to day activity before they were interrupted; gathering grain or herding cattle or selling items needed for day to day existence whether it was intended for in the home or in the field. There were cries from those who suffered or loss; others looked at what was left and got on with the struggle of rebuilding. Minsu and Jimin could not take their eyes off what had happened and the devastation it left behind. Nothing in their history books or anything Nam Jae Hoon said could have ever prepared them for the real life carnage and destruction of what they had just witnessed. Just as they were getting ready to go outside the helping "hand" that assisted them to hide at the moment of their arrival reappeared and moved them out of the dilapidated, tousled wooden hut. Being situated at a lower level on the plain and closer to the mountains, out of the way from the main village center the hut was spared the wrath and devastation of the soldiers, at least for now. Slowly Minsu and Jimin emerged frightened and disoriented, but with the help and gentle guidance of Nam Jae Young who vigilantly escorted the children into the broad open area of the village where they could regroup and regain their composure and introduce themselves to their new host. The gentle, soft, green pastoral setting lightly bedecked with short sparsely leafed trees contrasted sharply with the tall, placid, majestic mountains in the background and the laid to waste burning, devastated small village.

The children noticed that they were dressed not in their usual 21st century clothing attire but in clothing of the time wearing what looked like brightly colored "doll" outfits with long baggy sleeves and vivid colored slippers. Minsu looked at Jimin's clothes and then noticed that the shoes she was wearing were made of straw.

Nam Jae Young asked Minsu to see the sword that his brother Nam Jae Hoon had given him. Minsu slowly took the sword out of the sheath and held it up presenting it vertically towards the sun, like a victorious soldier displaying an award or trophy for everybody to see; glistening as it had when Nam Jae Hoon had given it to him. He looked at it, examined it very closely and after a few moments Nam Jae Young returned the sword and watched Minsu carefully slide it back into its sheath.

"Your journey has just begun and I will guide you on your way to Ms. Ok Eun Suk, matriarch of the Turquoise Palace of Korea Past and Present; a beautiful specimen of femininity, a Goddess whose beauty is only matched by her intelligence. Now you must get some sleep, we will begin our journey early tomorrow. You can stay near me in that wooden hut." As the children panned the area they could see a dilapidated, smaller, dark brown hut with one large gaping window. On the left side of the rectangular shaped wall there was an opening without any door. As the children entered the single room building a large stone fireplace to the left of the entrance which no doubt was the main source of heating and cooking also served as one of the walls. Situated on the right side of the hearth was a large cauldron with smaller pots and pans all neatly stacked up. There wasn't a bedroom or bathroom; the main living area was the only room since everything was centered on the fireplace and the heat it provided in the colder months. There was no floor but rather a hard stone surface and the furniture provided was a large brown wooden table in the middle of the room with two cots against the back wall that acted as beds. Tired and exhausted from a grueling day both children got into bed not even bothering themselves to get undressed since it was still quite chilly. The beds had no sheets or blankets and there wasn't any way to cover or secure the entrance. Both children looked at around their new surroundings and then at each other; the thrill of their new journey quickly turned to a look of fear, doubt and grief. Bathroom trips were rare and usually happened out the back behind a tree providing minimal privacy.

Early next morning before the sun was up the children were awakened by Nam Jae Young tapping on their shoulders. "Get up!" he said with a sense of urgency and haste. "The soldiers are coming back and we must leave quickly and be on our way." Minsu got up quickly, fearful of the impending threat and standing nearby looked on Jimin as she got on her feet still tired and dazed after a deep sleep and the suddenly startled by such an early alert. Quickly and quietly the three sneaked out under the cloak of a moonless night leaving the village on their way to a nearby thicket of trees. The galloping sound of the horses and their thundering hooves grinding up the soft earth grew louder and louder with every second sending a streak of fright and horror through all that could hear. The loud yells and screams of the riders grew to a fevered pitch as they ravaged and pillaged the village for yet another visit without any hesitation as to what destruction they could inflict on the peaceful villagers. A stronger scent of burning wood and grass filled the air again which filled Jimin and Minsu with a sense of urgency to get the sword to Ms. Ok Eun Suk as soon as they could. The urge to return to a more civilized, settled and peaceful time back in Sacheon was a driving passion. The thought and passing of Oonky had quickly been forgotten with their new surroundings and even life with their parents was a distant yearning memory. Life was nothing like anything they had ever imagined or experienced before. Constantly on their guard and ever vigilant the children had entered a new realm of existence with basic survival the key factor to their being. The amulet that they held so dearly and guarded with the utmost vigilance as their only means of return brought little comfort after the devastation they had seen and the fact there were no comforts and no chance to escape the circumstance that they were in. "Quickly, hide over here." blurted Nam Jae Young as the children made a quick dash behind the same small, empty, wooden cart. "Keep your heads down and don't make any noise." he whispered as the warriors got off their horses and looked around for any survivors. The children were at the zenith of their terror pitch, fearful for their lives and petrified at the thought of being detected in their shallow hollow behind the wooden cart. Two of the soldiers broke off from the group and expanded their search into the outlying areas just beyond the realm of the main population housing area or what was left of it. Two more of the warriors broke off from the larger band and started setting fires to less noticeable areas where the villagers had stored grain and hay. The silos lit up like bright candles illuminating the star sprinkled sky and the areas around them. The heat from the fire was almost enough to scorch the wooden cart they were hiding behind as they burned and burned and as the soldiers got closer and closer to their position of discretion and secrecy Jimin could almost feel her heart beating in her throat. Please leave us alone and let us get on with our journey so we can go home. Jimin thought to herself almost like a prayer to God fearing what might happen to them if they were ever discovered. Watching from their vantage point behind the cover of the trees they could see the heavily clad warrior's faces. Jimin watched in fear and disbelief and could almost sense that Minsu was repeating every word she said like a shadow mimicking every movement. And then suddenly, like a wayward wind changing direction the smaller group rejoined the others, mounted their horses and disappeared into the night under the twinkling star sprinkled sky. As the sound of the horses grew weaker and weaker Nam Jae Young, Minsu and Jimin emerged with caution and discretion from their hideaway. They all checked their possessions making certain that their pockets had their respective amulet halves and both felt comforted when they found they were still there. Tired and hungry since neither one of them had really slept for more than a couple of hours and now into their second day of hiding and living like outsiders, all three adventurers desperately tried to avoid the wrath of destruction and terror that was going on all around them. The kingdom that Nam Jae Hoon had fought so gallantly to save was annexed and no longer existed. Surrendering the sword to the mighty General Kim Yushin through Ms. OK Eun Suk would show his support for the new Kingdom of Silla. The General was actually born in the old Gaya Confederacy which had long since been annexed by the Kingdom of Silla. It was he who led the union of the Korean peninsula by Silla under the sovereignty of King Muyeol and King Munmu. Only the deity of education, beauty and the matriarch of the Palace, Ms. Ok Eun Suk could accept the sword as a gesture of humility from Nam Jae Hoon and present it to General Kim Yushin's module. As the journey "picked-up" the children took hold of the situation and paused at how their surroundings differed from what the Korea of their time looked like. "Sure doesn't look like where we are from, does it Minsu? It's Korea just a long time ago. I miss my comfortable bed and the Internet and Mom and Dad", Jimin lamented as she put her shirt on. "That's why we have to take care of this so we can get back home quickly." Minsu replied in a cynical tone. The sword that Nam Jae Hoon gave Minsu was always well guarded in a sheath at his side; constantly under the watchful placing of his right hand gently resting over handgrip. Within no time the three weary participants on a long and winding journey were back on their way to the majestic, opulent Turquoise Palace of Korea Past and Present; the home of Ms. OK Eun Suk. Along the way Minsu and Jimin noticed how open and remote everything seemed. What a difference 1,500 years can make to a country. Gone were the roads and smells and noises from the cars and buses and modern machinery; buildings were little more than wooden shacks and the soft, sweet smell of burning wood permeated the atmosphere. "Everything seems so much greener and cleaner. There aren't any schools or supermarkets here, not even a corner store-just fields and open space with the ubiquitous mountains, in the background." Minsu pointed out to Jimin. Occasionally a deer or snake would cross their path or a ring-necked pheasant or black grouse would startle them as it flew by. Jimin, at this stage, was only interested in one thing: getting back to her time and place-back to the future. They walked for days not knowing where they were going. Nam Jae Young was the guide and seemed to have a "built in compass" for direction and an ability to know where and when to stop to rest for a drink of water or camp for the night. Sometimes they would stop where they could out of necessity as the "better location" was occupied by a small band of cavalry soldiers and not available. He would also direct and inform Minsu and Jimin as to what was safe to eat and what to avoid. Nam Jae Hoon knew where to sleep whether it was under a group of trees for cover or sometimes out in the open if that was all that was available. Sometimes as they would pass from one village to another the townspeople and villagers would stop doing whatever they were doing and look but only briefly as the trio passed on by. Occasionally they would stop and find something simple and easy to eat whether it was being offered by a local friendly villager who would come out and offer it or whether they would have to go and get it by helping themselves. Both Minsu and Jimin found the staple diet of fermented fish, cabbage and rice offered by the local villagers to be revolting and barely palatable. Sometimes they would hold their noses and close their eyes as they consumed it.

They quickly discovered that the kimchi of the past, which was little more than radishes dipped in salt, was not the same as the kimchi of the present. "Too bad we have to eat." said Jimin, in a unhappy tone, "because this food is something I wish I could do without." "What a great chance to write our own history books; history as it is being made from our view. We even get to eat what people ate 1,500 years ago. This is healthy food" Minsu said to Jimin as they surveyed the area and paused to think about what was happening before them. "Our history teachers would give anything to be where we are, and sometimes I wish they were, just so they could see what we have to deal with. We could be experts on the subject." Jimin retorted with a tone of pride in her voice. Nothing could stop her feelings of homesickness and tiredness, wishing she were back at home longing to return to her more familiar time and surroundings. It was tough on both children to be in such a different situation having to act and think like adults and survive without the comforts and conveniences of the twenty first century and even tougher on Jimin because she was only 8 years old. Minsu, seemed to accept the challenges more willingly like a young man being the bearer of Nam Jae Hoon's sword, a tribute which he took with great pride and something that helped to raise his self esteem to lofty heights, something that also had a maturing effect on the young boy; gone were his boyish, childish actions, ideas and thoughts-now he was a man, he thought to himself, worthy of his new "rank" as "master of the sword", at least for this time. For the few days they had spent in their new "world" Minsu felt like there wasn't anything he couldn't do with just a little help from Nam Jae Young's expert abilities as a guide and teacher. Once Nam Jae Young got the children to the gate of the Turquoise Palace of Korea Past and Present they would be eligible, through their connection with him to present the sword to Ms. Ok Eun Suk.

After all 3 stopped momentarily for a drink and waited for Minsu to scrape the mud off his pants after he fell in a stream because he was not watching where he was going when he veered off, in a straight line like a soul being summoned to look at some strange fauna, Nam Jae Young proclaimed that the porthole to the Turquoise Palace of Korea Past and Present was near and would be reached within no more than two days. The children, in particular Jimin, were relieved at the thought of this journey coming to an end which sent a burst of optimism through her tired little body. For Minsu soon would be his moment of glory as even though they would both meet the matriarch together he would be the one that actually handed the sword over to the keeper of the Turquoise Palace. After 5 days of walking, foraging and sleeping wherever and whenever they could and avoiding the marauding warriors who seemed to come out of nowhere, many times without warning, the children could at least breathe a sigh of relief and know they would soon be back home with their mom and dad if everything went according to plan. Life would continue its same old routine; back to school at Donseong where they would have so much to tell; if people didn't believe what they said then they could demonstrate knowledge that they could not have possibly learned anywhere else but here. The children would be celebrities, not just in ancient Korea but also at home in modern Korea. After the brief rest and a chance to regain their poise the three were ready to start on what was to be the final leg of their journey as the end was now imminent and Jimin could breathe a sigh of relief to know that soon she'd be back in the comfort of her more familiar, peaceful way of life. Minsu had actually become accustomed to his new surroundings and welcomed the day to day challenges that came with his new found responsibility since it was he who had the task of getting the sword to its destination; quite a chore for a 10 year old boy. "We're almost there", Nam Jae Young declared in an exhausted out-of-breath huff after walking for what felt like an eternity into the dusk of the setting sun. With that, a sigh of relief spread across everybody as they gathered under a tree with a strange looking stone at the trunk: the focal point of Nam Jae Young's attention. "Give me the two halves of the amulet", Nam Jae Young said to the children upon which they both foraged through their pockets eventually presenting each half to him as he stood over what looked like an ordinary small piece of moss covered granite just barely protruding above the grass around it. Silently waiting with abundant looks of excitement from all attendants with the anticipation on their faces like the opening presents on Christmas morning, the children watched as Nam Jae Hoon waved the joined halves over the stone. All three looked on in amazement at the change happening right in front of them. In the time since Nam Jae Young waved the amulet over the stone, the stone started to slowly go through a gradual glowing change of color, starting with a bright shade of red and yellow all the way through the spectrum and beyond eventually stopping on a deep luminescent shade of turquoise. After standing back and watching the transformation and handing the amulet halves back to the children a turquoise beam of light began to emerge from the stone, narrow at first and then gradually increasing in width and height pointing straight upward like a brightly colored turquoise spotlight and blazing like a guiding light from the ground to the sky with silver and gold flashes at random points on the column. All three stood back and watched as the turquoise light increased in brightness, width and height climbing higher and higher into the bright blue sky eventually disappearing into the clouds and beyond. At no time did they ever feel any fear or terror; just wonder and amazement. As the beam grew to the degree where it was wide enough for the three to occupy it, Nam Jae Young took the children holding each one's hand and leading the way stepped into the dazzling pillar of light. The children were able to look out at their surroundings; a turquoise tint came over their eyes as they looked back at their former setting. Then, like an elevator ascending into the sky the beam, with all three travellers aboard, magically ascended disappearing into the clouds on yet another leg of their mystical, magical journey to return the sword to Kim Yushin's host and keeper of the Turquoise Palace of Korea past and present Ms. Ok Eun Suk. Shortly after arriving at their new destination the beam disappeared and presented the children and Nam Jae Young at the entrance to a brightly decorated turquoise and white gate with what appeared to be a building of mind boggling proportions in the background. Their surroundings consisted of a not easily distinguished horizon that appeared to back drop the palace which in itself was shrouded in white misty clouds with a bright golden beam that seemed to shine down on it embellishing the beauty of the surroundings creating a dazzling spotlight effect. It was a sight that neither of the children had ever seen before, not even in a fairy tale or fantasy book. Jimin turned to Minsu and asked, "Do you think this is heaven Minsu? It sure looks like what I imagine heaven to be." Minsu replied with a chuckle and then looked up at Nam Jae Young to see what he was staring at. Standing between them and the brightly colored, lavishly decorated white and turquoise gate flanked by large pillars of what appeared to be mother of pearl supporting ornate horizontal turquoise iron beams was a short, good looking specimen of what appeared to be a man in his early thirties dressed in traditional clothing of the period with a warm, welcoming smile on his face. "Hello" he greeted them with open arms and a warm welcoming smile. "My name is Mr. Been and I am your host to the gate to the Turquoise Palace of Korea past and present. Come with me now and I will guide you on your way through the gate to the Turquoise Palace of Korea past and present. There you will eventually meet the matriarch of the palace, Ms. Ok Eun Suk and present the sword of Nam Jae Hoon. "Anyway, how has your journey been? How did you like the way you got here?" Mr. Been asked with an ever present wide smile on his face. "We thought it was thrilling and very exciting. Better even than a trip to EVERLAND" replied Minsu. "I used to think EVERLAND was the best but not anymore. We would like to do it again, if we can, soon." Minsu said with a wide toothy smile. Jimin chimed in by saying that she had a feeling of warmth and comfort from the shaft of light; it was scary at first but thrilling and something like she'd never experienced before. All three of the travellers were transfixed by the beauty of the gate that Mr. Been guarded as they stood looking up at it only a few meters in front of the entrance. They were astounded and amazed by the intricacy of its ornate design with a stunning mixture of turquoise and mother of pearl; looming tall and majestic and only fit as an entrance to Ms. Ok Eun Suk, matriarch of the Turquoise Palace. As Nam Jae Hoon took the children by the hand and walked through the gate between the majestic, awe inspiring pillars with Mr. Been following closely behind all participants entered into a newer land, not totally unlike anything they had ever experienced up to this point in time. Jimin was the first to notice and comment that despite the outward appearance everything seemed normal. Gone were the white misty clouds and ground fog that seemed to enshroud the land when they first arrived; the bright golden sunbeams still bathed the palace in a shower of light which seemed to imposingly sit back on a hill of moderate elevation with what appeared to be a narrow grass covered walkway winding up to the main entrance. Looking around, the sites that one would normally associate with daily life would appear; a bird would fly by, a bee would land on a flower and the sun high in the sky was still shining brightly and the air felt a little warmer. "I don't know where we are now." Jimin commented to Minsu, "but it sure seems a lot safer than where we were. I don't see any of those large, ugly men on their horses riding around with fire on those long sticks that they used to carry." Even though Minsu had been given the superior task and responsibility of bearing the sword he told Jimin that apart from getting closer to the end of the journey he wanted to get rid of it because it was starting to rub his side when he walked, apart from being heavy. Jimin suggested that he should try putting it over his shoulder and let it hang down his back. After trying it for a time he found that it did indeed relieve the pain and chaffing. With the change in temperature, lack of proper nourishment and comfort Jimin had developed a slight cold which if not properly treated could lead to the flu or worse pneumonia. Minsu offered to let her wear his shoulder cover; a light cloth that draped over his shoulders and partly down his back, something that he had managed to pick up while walking through one of the villages on the way; a friendly villager offered it and he took it. Jimin thanked him and accepted his offer taking it with both hands draping it over her shoulders. As they continued along the grassy path and began to ascend the hill Minsu noted that to the left of palace and ata slightly lower elevation there were what appeared to be volley ball and tennis courts. Upon closer examination, the closer they got there were people playing both volleyball and tennis. Minsu noted that one of the volleyball players could be seen wearing what appeared to be an American Wonder Woman uniform. He couldn't quite see her face but from a distance she looked like every bit an Olympic athlete. What really surprised him and kept his attention was that she was playing against a team of six and winning every time. The closer they got to the palace the splendor and the magnificence of Ms. Ok Eun Suk's Turquoise Palace, just up ahead, all became so much more vivid. They all marvelled at the structure and the entrance which was adorned with vast amounts of white, turquoise and red stone with a large map of Korea in bright shades of blue, green and red marking the four kingdom divisions of Goguryeo,

Baekje, Silla and Gaya all in a half moon shape surrounded by a turquoise frame.

The framed image was situated on top of two enormous white ivory columns, each column flanking a large wooden door which had to be over 3 meters high barring any uninvited guests with two enormous one meter high vertical brass handles for holding. On the left side of the door the light from what appeared to be a small oil lantern which despite the bright light of the sun was still burning brightly with a small plume of black smoke streaming out the top like a thin black ribbon. "How are we going to get in?" asked Jimin. "Through that door right there, Jimin." replied Minsu. "Who is going to knock on the door?" she asked with apprehension and fear all across her face. Nam Jae Young, who had said very little the whole time they were on the road to the palace chimed in by saying that he was going to knock on the door. Because of his age and position as "leader" and since he was the one standing the closest, he obligingly walked over to the door and then paused, took a deep breath and with the confidence of a front line soldier gave three hard knocks, each one in rapid succession. After a brief pause, nothing happened and then looking up to the sky as if to wonder if anybody was home he focused his attention back on the door and repeated the action, "bang-bang-bang." A few moments passed and then there was some action. Suddenly all three paused as the heavy brown door began to slowly open. All three bystanders gasped, took a deep breath and watched with fear and excitement glued to the moment, waiting with anxiety approaching terror, afraid that they could have disturbed a malevolent power that could not be stopped as they uneasily anticipated what might have awaited them on the other side of the door. Minsu and Jimin could feel their hearts beating faster and faster as they held their breath. Slowly the door opened wider and wider. Jimin feared that maybe they had disturbed a malicious force, after what they had been through; she feared the worse and was horrified at the thought of what could be on the other side of the door. Nam Jae Young, eyes wide open standing stiff and firm in his place like a statue had a look of astonishment bordering on shock in direct sight of what was on the other side of the door. Just before the big brown door reached its maximum opening a small face suddenly appeared peaking out with a countenance like that of a cat or a rabbit, perhaps no more than one meter in height. Minsu and Jimin looked at each other and then stared at what appeared to be a large tabby cat with a long nose and wearing glasses. A smile flashed across the faces of Jimin and Minsu when it started to speak but their countenances quickly turned into surprise and wonder when it looked at them. "Welcome to the Turquoise Palace of Korea Past and Present. My name is Wonky. Please come in." With that invitation and Nam Jae Young leading the way all three adventurers followed through the entrance into the Turquoise Palace of Korea Past and Present. By this time Mr. Been had returned to his post at the gate. What was amazing, after Wonky's introduction, was he was able to walk on two feet. Wonky looked like a bright orange tabby cat but walked like a primate. As they passed through the entrance all three travellers looked in wonder and amazement at how the exceptionally gargantuan area was filled with action and movement from the sky high ceiling (which seemed to disappear into the sky) to the white (in some areas) marbled floor. The floor seemed to match the surrounding environment. Minsu and Jimin couldn't believe their eyes and even displayed some fear and anxiety at how children were leading, by a simple rope leash, large and in some cases dangerous animals like black and brown bears and tigers; beautiful young girls could be seen swinging back and forth on swings that were suspended on long brightly colored flowery ropes that extended all the way up to the ceiling which eventually seemed to disappear into the clouds. Flocks of birds, some in migration formation were seen flying overhead which made it seem more like an aviary depending on the location; some areas had modern city settings and yet others tropical jungle or polar tundra surroundings. Locations were covered in the surroundings indigenous to that area. As the children followed Nam Jae Young around the perimeter they noticed smaller areas set back and off to the side. Time and three dimensional spaces didn't exist with other basic laws of physics since any module could basically contain an area the size of a country or a universe and was large enough to contain the event or situation that helped to contribute to the history of Korea. The entrances were connected by doorways that contained some of Korea's great people like politicians, soldiers and kings. Passing through a doorway would take a person into that real life situation and one would experience it by seeing it in real time and what really happened in the situation. Minsu had always been a keen fan of Tae Kwon Do. Every Saturday morning he would get up early and go to the local kwan near the Sacheon Tourist hotel in downtown Sacheon. His instructor, Young Park was a native of Sacheon and very fond of all of his students. Even though Minsu would always take a few minutes and be late because he would like to stand out back and have a quick cigarette and a sip of soju with his school friends he was still, nevertheless, an ardent participant like many of the other Korean children encouraged and in some cases forced by their parents to attend and do well. Many of his friends at school were also interested in the art and were always keen to practice their newly learned skills with each other. Being able to see it performed by the original master and the way it evolved into what it is was an opportunity of a lifetime that nobody else could possibly have experienced. Minsu was anxious to pass through the porthole, to have an opportunity to learn from one of the greats in real time and see how it really evolved. Each porthole or module had an image above the entrance where an observer could look inside; the actual entrances or "portholes" were cloaked in a misty, foggy red, bluish, purple covering; much like an out-of-focus kaleidoscope. Any interested admirer would pass through the porthole. Minsu looked at it and then paused but was concerned about whether or not he would be able to get back. With a few more moments of deep thought, a few deep breaths and a leap of faith he passed through the porthole and in the flash of a light was in a real time module observing on a broad scale the life of General Choi Hong Hi and his contribution to the self defense art of Tae Kwon Do and considered by many, including himself, to be the father of the martial art. Minsu was amazed at how he could sit and watch the General in live real time action. It was like being at a movie and seeing it except it was all in real time. The General was conceived in Hwa Dae North Korea on November 09 1918, and was sent by his dad to study calligraphy under Han IL Dong who was additionally an "expert of Taek Kyon", the old craft of Korean foot battling (Park, 1993, p. 241). It is believed that after a turbulent incident over a gambling squabble with an enormous wrestler Mr Hu, in Korea fueled his determination to defend himself through training in the martial arts after Mr. Hu threatened to shred him piece by piece. General Choi is quoted as saying, "I would imagine that these were the techniques I would use to defend myself against the wrestler Mr. Hu, if he did attempt to carry out his promise to tear me limb from limb"(Park, 1993. p.242). Choi fled to Kyoto, Japan in 1937 to further his education (Goldman, A.L. 2002) (Park, 1993) and to escape the wrath of Mr. Hu. In Kyoto he concentrated his attention on English, science and karate keeping in mind in Kyoto he met a kindred Korean karate educator with the surname Kim who taught Choi this martial art workmanship. He likewise learned

Shotokan karate under Funakoshi Gichin. Park, S. H. (1993) Compelled to serve in the Japanese armed force which Choi didn't want to do amid World War 2 since Korea was a province of Japan, he objected to the Japanese presence in Korea; he was later ensnared in a defiance and sent to jail during which time he kept on honing hand to hand fighting. From 1946 to 1951 Choi was advanced in the Korean armed force from second lieutenant as far as possible up to Brigadier general and then in 1954 made lieutenant general . By 1955 there were numerous Kwans showing a mixed bag of Martial Arts frameworks under a wide range of marks. A portion of the abilities included Korean Yudo in light of Judo, Chinese hand battling and local kicking strategies obtained from Tae kyeon. Park, S. H. (1993) With an end goal to set up another name for this military workmanship a few understudies of the Chung Do Kwan, including Choi Hong Hi referenced a lexicon to concoct the name "Taekwon." Choi joined the components of Taekkyeon and Shotokan Karate to build up a military craftsmanship called Taekwon-Do which signifies "the method for hand and foot" and it was so named when pioneers of the biggest Kwan (Chung Do Kwan) and the military Oh Do Kwan met with prominent lawmakers and students of history with the end goal of setting up one martial art workmanship. The name picked on April 11 1955 was Taekwondo which spoke to the guideline of the considerable number of Kwans consolidated together. Choi established the Oh Do Kwan and held a fourth dan positioning in the Chung Do Kwan however because of claims of untrustworthiness Choi lost the rank and position in the Choi Do Kwon. Amid the 1960s, Choi and Nam Tae Hi drove the first experts of Taekwondo in advancing their military craftsmanship around the globe. (Park, S. H. (1993) In 1961 under the solicitation of the Korean government requested the Kwans to unite and the Korea Taekwondo Association (KTA) was shaped and General Choi was chosen as its first president. General Choi was conveyed of the nation as the diplomat for Tae Kwon Do. Tae Soo Do was utilized for a period however when Choi returned yet he demanded the name Taekwondo being utilized as a portion of the littler Kwans would not like to utilize the name Taekwondo. General Choi's despotic routines brought about rubbing among a portion of the other Kwan pioneers which constrained him to leave as President of the KTA. In 1972 after a protest by the South Korean government to acquainting the workmanship with North Korea Choi moved to Canada and in 1973 the South Korean government framed the WTF. In 1979 Choi moved to North Korea and was warmly welcomed by the North Korean government where they upheld him in spreading Taekwondo to the rest of the world. The General is considered to be the "Founder of Taekwondo" by the 5 International Taekwon-Do Federation organizations for his tremendous struggles and enormous contribution to the Martial Art after having reached the rank of 10th dan, Grand Master, Taekwon-Do (ITF) and a 2nd dan in karate. Having been promoted to Lieutenant General in 1954 in the Korean Army and being able to boast, just before his death, according to an article in **The Guardian** newspaper by Dakin Burdick through the ITF website 09 August 2002,(Burdick, 2002) " I am the man who has the most followers in the world". The young boy felt a sense of grief and loss when the general died June 15 2002 and that the martial art would never be as good again with the loss of the general, a true leader and man of determination and passion and somebody whom he admired for all his strength, courage and might. Minsu was still in the module after the General's display had finished and then watched it again, all in real time. Minsu wished that he could make such a contribution to the martial art or find something that he could do well and excel in. The experience with the general's module inspired him to do better and to never be late or tardy for classes again. The General is remembered as the founder and champion of TaeKwondo. (International Taekwon-Do Federation) Jimin was keen on discovering the module of Queen Seondeok (c. 600-647) who ruled from 632-647 C.E. of the Kim family. After Minsu went through the passageway to the module of General Choi Hong-Hi, Jimin strolled on to watch the teachings of Queen Seondeok, the first lady to rule Korea from the lofty rank of queen and who around 1500 years ago ruled Silla, one of the three kingdoms of Korea. Ruler Seondeok of Silla around 600 - 17 February 647 ruled as Queen of Silla, one of the Three Kingdoms of Korea, from 632 to 647. Lee, Bae-yong (2008). *Women in Korean History*. Ewha Womans University Press.Wollock, Jennifer G. (2011). *Rethinking Chivalry and Courtly Love*. Praeger. She was Silla's twenty-seventh ruler, and its first ruling ruler. She was the second female sovereign in East Asian history and energized a renaissance in thought, writing, and human expressions in Silla. Known as Princess Deokman before she was ruler and was by Sagi (an authentic record of the three kingdoms of Korea) the first of King Jinpyeong's (Chinp'yong) girl. Lee, Bae-yong (2008) Wollock, Jennifer G. (2011) Glancing around until she happened upon the module, Jimin immediately went through the opening and inside. Being the first female ruler and the second female ruler in East Asian history implied that ruler had a considerable measure of difficulties to meet from the to a great extent overwhelmed male ruler portion. For Jimin this was one of the high purposes of the entire adventure, to see a lady administer to a male overwhelmed society. In the wake of strolling through the "window" she could see, as Minsu did, the rundown of references and sources. Two of the most unmistakable or observable references were: Lee, Bae-yong (2008) Wollock, Jennifer G. (2011) Jimin strolled over and offered her regard to the two reference focuses and after that headed toward the survey territory and perceived how the ruler governed in a great extent male overwhelmed society. Her dad King Jinpyeong had an extreme choice to make as a consequence of having no male beneficiaries to succeed him. Her framework in the bone rank and her intelligence caused Jinpyeong to choose her as she was the eldest of his girls and in this manner next in line to succeed the throne. Lee. p. 137. There is, on the other hand, some contention encompassing this record as a few records do, to be sure, show that she was really much more youthful than her senior sister Princess Cheonmyeong. Who comprehends what the genuine story is, however, whichever way this happened did not dissuade or weaken the Queen's advantage in light of the fact that right now ladies had a certain level of control and impact as being so firmly associated with the Kings and officials of the time. Jimin dependably felt that females didn't number in the social progression positioning so this drew her consideration much all the more so in light of the fact that it was so surprising for a young lady to see a lady in such a high positioning as a ruler. Jimin saw that the ruler went to the throne at a troublesome time for Silla with its consistent clash and battles with Baekje and Goguryeo keeping her continually occupied. She was exceptionally shrewd and it is her insight and mind that kept Silla together and ready to protect itself against Baekje and Goguryeo; the other old kingdoms that likewise shared the landmass. Ruler Seondeok went to the throne after the passing of her dad King Chinp'yeong who kicked the bucket following 50 years of tenet. In her 14 years as ruler (632-647) she utilized her better mind manufactured organizations together and ties with different kingdoms. Jimin watched her with totally open eyes, fascinated at the way she carried on matters as she led and satisfied her convention as ruler in an extremely tumultuous time. One extremely troublesome circumstance emerged from inside which she could call her own kingdom when Bidam, considered the best rebel in Silla history, directed a resistance with the motto that, "female rulers can't govern the nation." (7. Silla and Wa) - *Bidam* Fortunately for her, the incredible General Kim Yushin (officer and head of the Imperial armed force) was on her side and as indicated by legend when a star fell which was seen by Bidam and his supporters as the destruction of the ruler's power. After finding out about this General Kim Yushin recommended that she fly a blazing kite to demonstrate that the star was back; set up and everything was OK. The ruler, similar to her dad and others was attracted to Buddhism and she saw a great deal of Buddhist sanctuaries being developed like the fruition and control of the development of the Hwangnyongsa pagoda; a nine story structure of more than 80 meters in stature; she additionally manufactured the "Star Gazing Tower" Jeon, Sang-woon. (1998) which was otherwise called Ch'omsongdae at Kyongju which is thought to be the first genuine planetarium or observatory in the far east. She was a kind and cherishing ruler who devoted much to the advancement and satisfaction and bliss of her kin. She reinforced ties with Tang China whereby she sent understudies there to get the best instruction conceivable. Her rule was much like the renaissance that happened in Europe amid the medieval times where advances and enhancements were executed in expressions of the human experience, writing and reasoning and she was the one to whom Jimin had so much confidence and admiration for; like a controlling light for a youthful susceptible young lady. The individuals were blessed to have had such a ruler, to the point that, Jimin pondered internally which just made her firm in her conviction that female rulers are pretty much comparable to their male partners. If more young ladies my age could encounter what I am encountering here in The Turquoise Palace, life may be a ton diverse and perhaps even better. Preceding entering the Turquoise Palace Minsu's enthusiasm for history or anything to do with the past was restricted in extension and significance. Be that as it may, since his time in the Turquoise Palace the impact of this genuine activity history as it was being made had a significant impact on the kid and he was pretty much as restless and inquisitive to see what was next in the line of intrigues and accomplishments like a gathering of youngsters with a free day go at EVERLAND. Every passageway to a module pursued a sequential succession around the royal residence in its request of event and every one of the three kingdoms had its own particular place in the arrangement around the border of this amphitheater of imagination and sight. The separations between the modules weren't generally the same. Minsu looked not too far along the verging on interminable divider and saw the module of King Gwanggaeto the Great (374-413) who ruled from 391-414 whose name signifies "Extremely Greatest King, Broad Expander of Territory" Bourgoin, Suzanne Michele, ed. (1998) and is likewise known by the names Yeongnak and Yeongnak Taewang. Just two rulers in Korean history had the sobriquet "great" appended to their names. He was the nineteenth ruler of Goguryeo . Not much sooner than the conception of Gwanggaeto the other kingdom, Baekje was the overwhelming kingdom in Korea subsequent to having soundly vanquished Goguryeo in 371 under King Geunchgo. Sosurim of Goguryeo who succeeded Gogukwon attempted to keep up an independent arrangement after his kingdom had been soundly crushed by Baekje. (Lee, Gil-sang. 2006). So as to keep any further attacks, Goguryeo attempted to frame a dependability expanding on conciliatory relations with Xienpei and Yuyeon China; Goguryeo ended up in a troublesome position with an intense Baekje at its doorstep.(Bourgoin, Suzanne Michele). Resolved to put a stop to the raiding impact of Baekje and recover a portion of the lost region, Gwanggaeto saw the need to reconstruct the Goguryeo's maritime armada and mounted force unit not long after taking the throne when his dad died in 391. The following year with a recently embraced title Yeongnak (Eternal Rejoicing) Emperor Gwanggaeto, one year after his dad passed on set out to assault Baekje with 50,000 mounted force where he additionally took 10 walled urban areas along the outskirt with Gorguryeo. Lord Asin counterattacked just to be crushed in 393 and then assaulted Goguryeo in 394 and again in 395 where he lost all times in the long run being pushed back to the Han River to Wiryeseong, Baekje's capital. Asin's behavior as pioneer went through uncertainty as Baekje now hinted at wavering. (Tongbuga Yŏksa Chaedan (Korea). 2007). After a year assaulting from the ocean which shocked Asin as he expected an area intrusion in 396, Gwanggaeto assaulted Wiryesong and destroyed the city by blazing 58 walled fortifications. (Another history of Korea. Cambridge, MA) Eventually, Asin surrendered to Gwanggaeto with the mortification of giving his sibling over to Goguryeo as detainee for a stipulation to guarantee that he would keep up his standard over Baekje. Revenge more likely than not had been something that Gwanggaeto delighted in light of the fact that now he could assert an unmistakable point of interest over Baekje on the Korean peninsula subsequent to having recovered every one of that was lost at the season of his introduction to the world. (Yi, Ki-baek. 1984) Gwanggaeto's prosperity more likely than not pulled in devotees in light of the fact that in 400 Silla looked for help from Goguryeo after an organization together of the Gaya Confederacy and Baekje. Gwanggaeto soundly figured out how to vanquish the Japanese, Gaya and Bakje constrains subsequent to assaulting them with 50,000 mounted force units. This inevitably made Silla and Gaya submit to his power. Minsu was astounded and appreciated the quality and charge with which

Gwanggaeto had the capacity put down any uprisings and recover the lost Goguryeo domain. He contemplated Asin and every one of the times he attempted to assault Gwanggaeto and how he was vanquished come what may. Later in 402 Silseong came back to Silla; however Goguryeo kept up its impact over Silla. At the season of Gwanggaeto's demise in 413 at just 39 years of age by death from infection Goguryeo had vanquished 64 walled urban communities and 1,400 town. Bourgoin, Suzanne Michele, ed. (1998). Gwanggaeto controlled a colossal segment of the Korean promontory even by all accounts between the Amur and Han waterways with 66% of Korea, Manchuria and parts of Russia and inward Mongolia. Korea would never see region of such a terrific scale like, to that point again. Subsequent to leaving the module Minsu was resolved to some time or another to see the landmark that was raised in 414 in southern Manchuria. It likewise made him understand that things in life don't come effortlessly and that it's a consistent battle against the powers that come into our presence. In the wake of leaving the module Minsu however that he might want to see the landmark that recorded his when he returned to his time, which was raised in 414 in southern Manchuria. The entire experience inside the Turquoise Palace was an environment that defied the natural laws of physics. Indeed Nam Jae Hoon was the first stage of this whole adventure; a fantasy of gigantic proportions. Minsu being the curious little boy he was attempted to touch one of the walls to see what the perimeter was really made of since it seemed to have no real definition or substance to it. From a distance the walls appeared as a hazy shade of light turquoise but as he walked around the palace the walls would change in color from bright red to yellow or green depending on the location; every time he got closer to touch what appeared to be a wall or the perimeter sometimes it would move away; other times his hand would disappear and then only reveal itself as he pulled it away. The sounds that filled the area were those that accompanied every action that fit the location. Minsu noticed that as he passed Yi Sun-Sin's module the sounds of cannon and gun fire along with men screaming and yelling naval commands could be heard. The whole palace was an assortment of sights and sounds. Jimin's growing interest in history found her standing near the center of the palace focusing on Korean wildlife where she observed, first hand, some of the animals that have been forced out of their habitats or extirpated like the Siberian tiger and the Japanese sea lion with the passage of time and human encroachment. Other animals like the Roe deer and brown bear could be seen moving freely in their own surroundings without any fear or threat from their human neighbors. As Jimin stood on a small mound she wondered at this surreal setting and what her science teacher Mr. Kang would think if he could see it and how he might react to her detailed firsthand account of all this wildlife; would he believe me, she wondered. During the earlier three kingdoms period which lasted from 18BC to 935AD both children tried to explore as many modules as possible. As they are both from the southern locale and since Nam Jae Hoon was an officer from this territory they needed to investigate the Gaya Confederacy (AD 42-532) module and see what prompted its downfall. Every one of the occasions and crossroads in Korean history could be investigated from the grandness of the Turquoise Palace since it contained Korea; over a wide span of time. Entering the module the youngsters could see, regardless of the distinction in time, what they believed were well known sights around the Gimhae since territory they have a close relative who lives there. Arranged in the Nakdon River bowl on the southern eastern shoreline of South Korea, Gaya was conceived out of the alliance of the Samhan period in Korean history. Gaya was a mix of little city states (Barnes, Gina L. (2001)

with individual strategies that made up the alliance of six inexactly sorted out chiefdoms that in the long run changed into the six Gaya bunches. Legend makes them according to (Barnes 2001:180-182) "the year AD 42 saw six eggs dive from paradise with a message that they would be best." Suro who was one of them went ahead to turn into the lord of Geumwan Gaya and the other 5 young men went ahead to establish the remaining Daegaya, Seongsan Gaya, Ara Gaya, Goryeong Gaya, and Sogaya. Both youngsters had the capacity to see, from their vantage point, how the recent piece of the third century saw a move from the Byeonhan (Sin, K.C. (2000) alliance to Gaya with an increment in military action persisted from the Buyeo Kingdom with its more controlled, military style of standard. Since the kingdom was situated on the alluvial pads of the Nakdong waterway valley, a territory rich in normal assets, for example, farming, angling it did a considerable measure of exchange. Minsu and Jimin review how their close relative discussed their uncle and how he functioned as an angler in this locale much sooner than Minsu and Jimin were even conceived. Being a district rich in iron and meta, Gaya nations did a considerable measure of exchange with Kyushu, Japan sending out iron mineral and iron defensive products to Baekje and the Kingdom of Wa in the Yamato period; the innovation of Gaya was significantly more progressed than anything that could be found in any of the Japanese traditions. (Lee, Peter H & Wm. Theodore De Bary) (John Whitney Hall (1998). The Gaya nations shaped an alliance that focused in Gimhae in the second and third hundreds of years. As indicated by André Schmid (2002) and (Lee, Peter H & Wm. Theodore De Bary) Gaya was truly only a military station of Japan amid the Yamato period (300-710) which was one of the reasons why the Japanese defended the intrusion of Korea (1910-1945). This thought has been minimized as the Japanese administration wasn't even sufficiently solid to overcome Gaya. The Gaya Confederacy collapsed because of the weight of Goguryeo between AD 391 and 412 and in the long run broken down after an overwhelming thrashing by Silla in 562 as discipline for helping Baekje in a war against Silla. After the Gaya experience both kids felt considerably closer to Nam Jae Hoon getting somewhat more knowledge into his battle against some imposing neighbors and restricting opportunities. There was no plan or pattern to their exploring. Whatever was nearby or happened to interest them was where they would go. There was so much to see and learn. They were still youngsters and inquisitive. The following module was one that they both felt they ought to see since it truly prompted the establishing of the Goryeo Kingdom by Taejo. Prior to the unification of the Korean promontory under Goryeo there was a three kingdom period between 50 BCE and 935CE. These three kingdoms (Silla, Baekje and Goguryeo) were always warring with one another. Both youngsters remained before Taejo of Goryeo's module and felt propelled to go inside. In the wake of going through the window Jimin lost her breath at the introductory stun of her new surroundings; she was startled by how primitive it all appeared to be such a long time ago; how troublesome it should all have been. Taejo who was otherwise called Taejo Wang Geon and was naturally introduced to a genuinely well-to-do trader family on January 31, 877. Taejo Wang Geon was the organizer of the Goryeo Dynasty which managed Korea from the tenth to fourteenth Century AD; 태조 (in Korean). (Doosan Encyclopedia) Taejo ruled from 918-943; a shaky time without a doubt subsequent to a large number of the neighborhood pioneers and crooks were inconsistent with Queen Jinsung. (Doosan Encyclopedia). His dad Wang Ryung was an effective trader at Songdo who turned out to be truly well off doing exchange with China through the control he had on the Ryesong River. Taejo's falsehood got off to an extreme begin in the shaky period under Queen Jinsung. As she was not able to enhance the life of her kin a hefty portion of the neighborhood pioneers revolted and two of them were Gung Ye of the northwestern region of Silla and Gyeon Hwon of the southwest district These agitators picked up a great deal of force against the ruler. Gung Ye saw what an extraordinary military authority Wang Geon was and soon elevated him to general) (Doosan Encyclopedia) notwithstanding set so far as to call Wang Geon "sibling". Because of some military triumphs and battles he picked up prevalence with the individuals in light of his authority and liberality. Selected in 913 (Doosan Encyclopedia) of the recently established Taebong its ruler Gung Ye began to mistreat his subjects and even executed a few ministers or anyone who contradicted his religious perspectives. In a rebellion four officers plotted to oust the ruler which they did in 918 when they had him executed; he dropped out of support with a great deal of his subjects over his religious contentions and turned out to be extremely disliked. Subsequent to advancing Buddhism as Goryeo's religion after he renamed Taebong, Goryeo he attempted to recover control by looking for cooperation which with a percentage of the neighborhood families instead of attempting to overcome them. After the last ruler of Silla, King Gyeonsun surrendered the greater part of his property to Taejo in 935 and later in 936. Taejo drove a successful crusade against Singeom which later got to be Baekje which inevitably surrendered to Taejo. In the end every one of the three kingdoms Bakje, Silla and Balhae stopped to exist in the meantime. Taejo's unification of the Korean promontory in 936 was a complete unification that saw the development of one state (Doosan Encyclopedia) where the populace of Korea saw no progressions until 1948 upon the division of Korea into North and South. In the wake of survey the turbulent and unsteady times of Taejo the youngsters both trusted immovably that some time or another Korea would be one state again and under one pioneer. The abbreviated name of Goguryeo was embraced by Goryeo and this was the manner by which Korea got its name in English. The kids were in addition exceptionally intrigued, backpedaling further in time, of a questionable figure amid the melting away days of Goguryeo,(37-668) one of the three kingdoms of old Korea. Yeon Gaesomun (603-666) was a persuasive and questionable figure in the" sundown" days of the Goguryeo kingdom. (Samguk Sagi, vol 21) Born of high class and position in Goguryeo he was the first and final child of Yeon Taejo. He is associated with his contentions and dealings with the Tang administration of China under Li Shimin and his child Emperor Gaozong. (Old Book of Tang, vols 3 p199). Considered by customary Korean history books as a coldblooded and merciless pioneer whose defiant approaches and activities prompted the death of Goguryeo, another perspective proposes that his triumphs in guarding Goguryeo from the rage of China earned him acclaim and admiration, absolutely from the Korean antiquarian Shin Chaeho. In Shin's perspective "Yeon Gaesomun was the best saint in Korean history." Despite his strategies and way for managing rivals, numerous Korean researchers laud his recognition as a trooper, statesman and scholarly. The perspectives are fluctuated as some Chinese and Japanese researchers unequivocally oppose this idea. (Nihon Shoki, Fist year of Empress Kōgyoku (642) King Yongyu, in the winter of 642 wanted to have Yeon murdered as he was afraid for his general; he truly didn't recognize what to make of him yet realized that he couldn't believe him. An arrangement was brought forth by his authorities to have Jeon executed however when gotten some answers concerning this he held a rich meal and had one hundred of the restricting priests and authorities welcomed whereby Jeon murdered all of them.

Yeon discarded the lord's body without legitimate function . Yeon Gaesomun set Yeongnyu's nephew, Bojang, on the throne the child of the more youthful sibling of the previous King Yeongyu. Bojang did simply offer authenticity to Yeon's military manage as a "manikin" lord. In the wake of putting Bojang on the throne Yeon announced himself Dae Magniji or Generalissimo . (Samguk Sagi, vol. 21) Under weight from Yeon, Bojang received Taoism and made it the national religion despite the fact that Buddhism had been the official religion up to this time. (New Book of Tang, vols. 2, 220) Many of the authorities that Yeon had killed in the Coup d'état favored submission with Tang China; Yeon was one of those military hard-liners who pushed meeting and a harder position against Tang China. Yeon at first took a short discretionary position with China however this was all only appearance as he utilized the time to plan for the Tang attack. He bolstered Taoism and even sent emissaries to the Tang court in the trust of increasing some Taoist sages(Zizhi Tongjian, vols. 197, 198). At the point when Goguryeo propelled new intrusions of Silla the relations with Tang China decayed. In 645 Emperor Taizong's prominent military discernment empowered him to vanquish some Goguryeo outskirt strongholds when the Goguryeo/Tang wars began yet his armed force was met with setback after setback.. Taizong's failure to overcome Goguryeo after two more endeavors in 661 and afterward after another annihilation for Taizong in 662 demonstrated Taizong's captivation for needing to vanquish Goguryeo. The Goguryeo populace and economy were extremely debilitated by the consistent Tang attacks and in 668, 8 years after Yeon's passing, Goguryeo broke apart. Similarly as with numerous different assumes that achieved a ton of progress, Yeon was seen as a disputable figure in Korean history. Still depicted by some Silla and Tang sources as an underhanded and self important despot yet his fundamental objective was to stop Tang powers and protect Goruryeo from intrusion. After Yeon's passing in 666 Bojang was not able to retake control of the nation which had been shredded by a progression battle by Yeon's children. In the wake of leaving the Yeon Gaesomun module both kids returned away with a thought that he was heartless and unforgiving, however both kids understood that this was the means by which life was more than 1000 years back and Yeon did whatever he could to hold Goguryeo together. Under steady dangers against the other 2 kingdoms in Korea and China he was a true "pathfinder" and a decided pioneer. Both kids left with a sentiment how remorseless, eager and force hungry Yeon Gaesomun had been yet at the same time somebody deserving of admiration, in light of the fact that he was the author of the Goguryeo Kingdom. King Bojang was the last of King Dongmyeong of Goguryeo's ancestors to rule Goguryeo and did not receive a temple name. "We really got two parts of Korean history in one module in Yeon Gaesomun's module with King Bojang's involvement." noted Jimin. After the children exited the module Minsu left Jimin standing at the entrance of Yeon Gaesomun's module whereby he returned a few moments later with a must see look of excitement all over his face. "Come and look at this now." Minsu said to her as he came out from behind where she was standing giving a little tug on her coat startling her as he seemed to appear out of nowhere. "I have recently discovered where Admiral Yi Sun Sin's Yi Sun-sin's (Hangul: 이순신; hanja: 李舜臣; April 28, 1545 – December 16, 1598) module is." exclaimed Minsu. Rapidly both youngsters headed toward the module and without a second thought went inside. With a 10,000 foot perspective looking down on a cutting edge circumstance of the highlights of his profession and what truly happened, the youngsters had the capacity to witness how the considerable Admiral utilized different strategies to draw the forceful Japanese naval force into a tight strait or a range further bolstering his good fortune and afterward observed how the Admiral demolished their armada. What set the Admiral separated from the rest was the way that he never had any maritime preparing or even took part in any maritime battle however all things considered succeeded in turning into one of only a handful couple of chiefs of naval operations to never lose a fight. To supply the armed force in its drive up the Korean landmass the Japanese armed force relied on its naval force for supplies. Chief naval officer Yi Sun Sin is a saint of huge extents, with an extremely extraordinary place in the hearts of most Koreans for the way he chivalrously vanquished the Japanese with 23 triumphs and repulsed many, many invasions. Minsu could see that Jimin was pretty much as intrigued by the splendid military strategies of the Admiral as he was which astonished him, at first. Chief of naval operations Yi Sun-sin A brief diagram of his life and accomplishments. Chief of naval operations Yi Sun-sin at Koreanhero.net. With his splendid maritime strategies, the greater part of this found progressively since the kids could really witness from their vantage point how it all happened. Yi was really conceived in the refined neighborhood of Geonchondong, Seoul however invested some energy in Asan get ready for the military exam of Asan which he inevitably succeeded in going in 1576 at the age of 32; a stallion riding mischance frustrated his advancement after he broke his left leg. (Chief naval officer Yi Sun-sin at Koreanhero.net). An essential occasion happened in his life when he met Ryu Seongryong (류성룡; 柳成龍; 1542–1607),who was in charge of the military and who turned out to be a significant companion with his backing of Yi amid the Japanese intrusions of Korea (1592-1598). Hawley, Samuel (2005). The adventure for the youngsters and the Admiral really began in Japan which was another reward for them since neither one of them (the kids) had ever been to Japan. The war mongering

Toyotomi Hideyoshi referred to through designation as the "Napoleon of Japan " had a goal-oriented streak in the wake of getting through the Warring States Period in 1592. Hawley, Samuel (2005). With a large number of prepared to-battle Samurai warriors close by he needed to attack Ming, China. The least demanding or most effective route for him to do this was to take his troops and experience Joseon Korea and utilize the peninsula for his forward base. This period came to be known as the Japanese intrusions of Korea or the Imjin War which kept going from 1592-1598. Hawley, Samuel: The Imjin War. With his advancement to Naval Commander the chief of naval operations set out with the undertaking of enhancing and overhauling the Korean Naval Force. He streamlined the regulatory framework, and made moves up to the weapons and even attempted to enhance the control of the Korean mariner. Naval commander Yi Sun-sin at Koreanhero. net. The Admiral is most noted for his 23 triumphs against the Japanese intruders and particularly for the Battles of Myeongnyang and Hansan do Island which are both thought to be the most well known fights. His vicinity on the oceans made the Japanese officers intensely mindful to the need to dispense with him since Hideyoshi Toyotomi should have been have the capacity to control the supply lines. The Admiral was a convincing pioneer and would never request that his troopers do something that he wouldn't do himself. As a major aspect of his arrangement the Admiral revamped and enhanced the Turtle Ship which was truly the precursor to the heavily clad warship. One of the Japanese strategies was to board the boat and take part close by to hand battle; the spiked structure of the Turtle Ship made this incomprehensible. As a splendid strategist everything must be arranged for war subsequent to legitimate planning would quite often ensure achievement. The Korean naval force pontoon was likewise preferable arranged for war over its Japanese partner: the

Joseon panokseon boats were much sturdier than the Japanese sends and were additionally better equipped with 20 guns contrasted with the Japanese 2. Amid the Battle of Myeongnyang (Park, Yune-Hee 1973) his power was one twenty fifth (around 13 ships) the span of what the Japanese armada had however that didn't make a difference; knowing the streams and the south bank of Korea did make a difference and attempted to his advantage when he utilized this learning to vanquish the Japanese intruders and smash their armada. (Hawley, Samuel 2005 The Imjin War) On the morning of August 14 1592 amid the Battle of Hansan island, which was the first in the Admiral Yi's third crusade furthermore thought to be the third biggest maritime fight in maritime history, the Japanese armada under Wakisaka Yasuhara lay at grapple in the Gyeonnaeryang Strait. Wakizaka's armada comprised of 73 boats of different diverse sorts which turned out to be an impressive array. Be that as it may, to their hindrance the Japanese ships conveyed few guns contrasted with their Korean partners. Naval commander Yi by differentiation had just 57 boats under his control which comprised of the 70-100 foot long triple deck Panokseon. (Turnbull, Stephen 2002) These boats utilized shields around their decks as a methods for protection. The Admiral ordered six of his Panokseon ships, which was the standard warship of the time amid the seven years war, to draw the Japanese out of the channel into untamed waters. The Japanese administrator Wakisaka drew-up his stays and sought after the Korean pontoons into untamed waters. Turnbull, Stephen. 2002 Lying in hold up close Hansan-do was an extra 50 Korean ships whereby the Admiral composed them fit as a fiddle. Wakisaka attempted to board the Korean delivers yet was unsuccessful because of the Korean ships' shields and reinforcement. (Hawley, Samuel 2005) The concealed Japanese armada was peppered with gun shoot, flaring bolts and flintlock discharge from both sides.

The gently defensively covered Japanese boats were no match for the Korean armada with its guns. Smoke streamed out of the guns and discharge were fed underneath the winged serpents' mouths on the boats which were an alarming sight; by mid evening 47 of the Japanese boats were at the base of the sea and 12 more had been caught. (Hawley, Samuel 2005) The Imjin War: Approximately 8,500 Japanese mariners were executed and the Admiral didn't lose a solitary ship; his setbacks numbered just 19 murdered and 100 harmed. The Admiral's triumph at Hansan Island adequately put an end to Hideyoshi's fantasies of overcoming Ming China. Turnbull, Stephen. 2002, In spite of his presentation of virtuoso adrift, Admiral Yi needed to bear some huge difficulties in his own life which never meddled or reduced his devotion to his reason: he was a genuinely commendable individual. Confronted with a ruler who attempted to slaughter him his unfaltering dependability to Korea and the individuals empowered him to be post mortem given the title of Chung Mu (Duke of Loyalty and Chivalry) after his demise at 54 years old in 1598 in the wake of being struck by a shot. (Chief naval officer Yi Sun-sin at Koreanhero.net) After the kids saw the Admiral's life and the highpoints of his vocation, a post mortem applause book appeared at the passage to the passageway loaded with awards and respects structure individuals who genuinely appreciated and regarded him. Chief of naval operations George Alexander Ballard of England (The Influence of the Sea on The Political History of Japan (1921) contrasted him with the considerable Admiral Nelson of Trafalgar for his splendid strategies and moves . Lieutenant Commander Kawada Isao noted in his book distributed in 1908: "Chief naval officer Yi's solid identity characteristics were all deserving of our profound respect." Admiral Tetsutaro Sato of the Japanese Navy applauded him as a "... really incredible leader and an expert of maritime strategies more than 300 hundred years prior." He was additionally made Chungmugong which is a high military honor and the longest suspension connect in Korea was named after him. Both kids had tears in their eyes when they cleared out the module, not out of pity but rather for the love and admiration for this awesome individual who did as such much for Korea and gave all that he had, even his life at last and who in spite of his setbacks never fizzled or faltered from his unwaveringness to the ruler and the individuals. Since Minsu and Jimin were at the Turquoise Palace and time had no effect they wanted to see as much of Korean history as they could; they never realized how fun it could all be. "How about we check whether we can discover King Seonjo's module since he was the King at the season of Yi Sun Sin?" encouraged Jimin. "That'll finish everything to know amid the Admiral's opportunity." she included. We've as of now seen the Japanese side with Toyotomi Hideyoshi. Ruler Seonjo's module wasn't too far away from the Admiral's so both youngsters rushed inside. The youngsters sat and observed all the significant occasions in the King's life and were interested to know why he was known as the "distraught" lord. Lord Seonjo was the fourteenth King of Joseon Korea. He was conceived a sovereign: Yi Yeon in Seoul and child of the "Incomparable Prince of the Court" Deokheung Daewongun on November (a few references say December 26) 1552. (Korean) Seonjo at Doosan Encyclopedia. Amid his rule as ruler numerous progressions occurred in Korea both of his doing and some not from his doing. The lord was delegated in 1567 at just 16 years old after the demise of King Myeongjeong who kicked the bucket with no beneficiary. (Seonjo at Doosan Encyclopedia) (Seonjo at Encyclopedia of Korean Culture). Ruler Seonjo had numerous great aims as lord with the trust of enhancing the lives of the individuals and enhancing the nation after the politically degenerate tenet amid the rule of Yeonsangun and King Jungjong. Both youngsters appreciated his great goals of selecting a gathering of new researchers to high office with an end goal to supplant the individuals who had become degenerate. He advanced Sarim researchers who had endured different types of oppression somewhere around 1498 and 1545 furthermore proceeded with the politcal changes of King Myeongjong. (Seonjo at Doosan Encyclopedia) He was resolved to upgrade the common authority capability exam and verify that they had a broad information of history and legislative issues with the Confucian ethical quality rule consolidating an extensive variety of orders; the old one truly just centered around writing. (Seonjo at Doosan Encyclopedia) (The Academy of Korean Studies) Purging the old and "setting the stage for the new," the King set out on a wide scope of recommendations to clear up the oversights of the past. On the other hand, in 1575 Sim Ui-gyeom and Kim Hyowon the two researchers called to the administration, one of whom was a relative of the ruler and exceptionally traditionalist. (Sim Ui-gyeom at Doosan Encyclopedia) the researchers split into two groups which would have destroying impacts for the nation; the lord was attempting to situated the course for the nation calling for liberal changes. What came to be known as the East-West fight went on for a long time from 1575-1592. Both researchers, who bolstered the lord, lived in the same neighborhood. (Korean) Seonjo at Encyclopedia of Korean Culture). The preservationist group under Sim and the liberal group under Kim came to be known as the eastern and western divisions. In the first place the King upheld the traditionalist side in light of the fact that they bolstered the ruler yet their gradualness to grasp a portion of the changes supported by the lord gave the eastern division, under Kim, a chance to ascend to the top which essentially implied the ruler needed to move to the side. This two group framework went on for a long time and in the long run cut down the tradition. To aggravate matters even the easterner group isolated into the northern and southern group: the northerner group which was exceptionally radical and more so than the southern group partitioned even again as they got to be "stalled" over more issues. (Korean) Seonjo at Encyclopedia of Korean Culture. These poliical issues debilitated the nation and since the military was one of the issues on the plan this extremely debilitated it as well. Another component was the issue with the ascent of Japan and the Jurchens (tenants of Manchuria) with their imperialistic intentions. Yi who was a nonpartisan traditionalist encouraged the ruler to modify the military, to go about as an obstruction against the Jurchens and the Japanese. One progressive encouraged the revamping of the military which wasn't an awful thought at the time considering Korea had some really capable neighbors. The thought was pounded by both groups believing that peace and congruity would keep going forever. Both the Japanese and the Jurchens grabbed the chance to advance their intrigues which would prompt destroying results for the Korean landmass. (The Academy of Korean Studies, Korea through the Ages Vol. 1 p189-p195). Confronted with tremendous issues in managing the new dangers and after the unification of Japan numerous Koreans were concerned about the fact that their nation would turn into a settlement of Japan. The southern danger from Toyotom Hideyoshi was a far more prominent risk particularly when the Japanese pushed north to seize Seoul in 1592. As the Koreans arranged for the inescapable, the Japanese were making flintlocks and assembling warriors from the nation over. After Seoul was taken by the Japanese the lord had no real option except to leave moving to Pyongyang and after that onto Uiju. The kids came to understand that the lord took a risk and settled on the wrong choice. The individuals who concentrated the northern front against China minimized the Japanese risk which was much more genuine. Things changed a little for the lord when Admiral Yi Sun sin and his Turtle Boats crushed the Japanese supply lines and hindered any possibilities of triumph for the Japanese after a dazzling triumph for Korea at the skirmish of Haengju. Seoul was retaken amid peace transactions with Japan, however, the royal residences had been smoldered to the ground by individuals who had lost trust in the administration. When he came back to Seoul, Seonjo repaired one of the old royal residences and renamed it Deoksugong. (Won Gyun at Encyclopedia of Korean Culture). The ruler did not appreciate a burst in ubiquity that one would expect for a successful ruler. The individuals were ravenous and tired yet more regrettable was the political factionalism of east and west, north and south persevered. Japanese attacks of Korea 1592–1598 at Doosan Encyclopedia (Korean) Seonjo at Doosan Encyclopedia. Agitated and dampened and even discouraged, King Seonjo turned over his obligations to the crown sovereign. In 1608 the lord passed on with the nation in a moderate recuperation frustrated by two effective neighbors: Japan and Manchuria. He made a bet and lost, however, risks are that regardless of which decision he made whether to counter the Manchurian or Japanese danger had no effect as both sides were resolved and imposing. The King ought to be associated with his great aims and what great he did was just for the benefit of the individuals and his certifiable sympathy toward enhancing their lives. Both youngsters returned far from the King's module distress stricken and even a bit discouraged at how out of line and pitiless life can be now and again. Looking around and not a long way from where they were Minsu saw the module of King Seongjong, the ninth ruler in the Joseon Dynasty. "We should go inside this one Jimin. I have heard a great deal about King Seongjong, and I believe it's great to see him since Mom meets expectations in a region that saw some of his impact by supporting aining and learning." Both kids went into the module and unobtrusively saw in surprise and hush at yet another glad crossroads in Korea history. Everything appeared to be so genuine and there were times when both kids tried to touch the members. King Seongjong showed up at just 13 years of age subsequent to King Yejong dying in 1469 with no beneficiaries. He did, however have a little assistance from his mom Queen Insu (Great Royal Dowager Queen (대왕대비) and grandma Queen Jeonghee who managed for his sake till he came to 20. Lord Seongjong, who ruled from 1457-1494 was a talented and able ruler portrayed by how the national economy developed and flourished by usage of the Grand Code of Managing the Nation (Gyeonggukdaejeon); he additionally supported Confucian researchers. (Kang, Jae-eun, and Suzanne Lee. 2006). The majority of the laws set around lords Taejong, Sejong and Sejo helped Seongjeong's rule run easily. Ruler Sejo who truly settled the code of law in 474 saw King Seongjong which was initially requested by years before it was culminated and commanded. Gyeonggukdaejeon was a bona fide endeavor to set a "seat mark" for setting up a full legitimate arrangement of administration as a complete code contained each law, demonstration, custom, statute discharged following the late Goryeo Dynasty to the Joseon Dynasty. "경국대전(經國大典), Gyeonggukdaejeon" (in Korean and English). The Academy of Korean Studies. In spite of all that they had seen and every one of their endeavors there was a persistent mission to discover General Kim Yushin's module since it was truly the reason in respect to why they were in the Palace; tragically regardless of how hard they looked they were not able to discover General Kim Yushin's module. "How about we observe King Hyegong of Silla. I never forget my history instructor discussing why he was executed; however I simply need to check whether it's valid." said Minsu. As the kids went inside the module they were astounded at the amount he acted like a lady. Jimin thought she was watching a young lady and was flabbergasted at how youthful he looked when he went to the throne. Hyegong of Silla, ruled from 765-780 and was the 36th leader of Silla and the last relative of King Muyeol to sit on the throne. He didn't adjust well to being ruler at 8 years old. His wicked life kept the castle in confusion and he confronted numerous uprisings by high authorities like Kim Daegong and a couple of others in 768, 770 and 775. Hyegong was feminine and was depicted as a man by appearance yet a lady by nature. He was murdered in the April 780 defiance that raged the royal residence since his subordinates couldn't endure his gentility. "I don't imagine that murdering some person for being like that is an extremely useful thing to do or going to unravel anything." regretted Jimin. "We're all distinctive. Rather than murdering him why didn't they simply give him another thing to do? He was probably harmless." she included. After both kids left the module they were still inquisitive and resolved to discover the module of General Kim Yushin. At that point and out of the blue with no notice and what's more, in a split second, as though someone had killed a switch or pulled the fitting on a feature show, everything went calm and solidified in position, similar to a still picture in suspended liveliness. The sounds from the feathered creatures flying over head and every one of the creatures in the royal residence all of a sudden went calm; solidified in time and position. Just Nam Jae Young, Minsu and Jimin had the capacity talk or move and witness the change that spoke the truth to happen with the entire circumstance. At that point from far above like a twinkling star in the morning sky; a brilliant shining bit; a kaleidoscope of numerous shades of red and green, blue and yellow with turquoise and pink flashes on a hard shape to characterize protest gradually showed up from the highest point of the royal residence furthermore, plunged to their area stopping from all movement just a couple meters above where they were standing, just before. "This must be what we have been sitting tight for. The hotly anticipated landing of Ms Ok Eun Suk." whispered Minsu. "I think this is in reality Ms. Ok Eun Suk and now we can give her the sword; our adventure is nearing to an end." Both youngsters were in a stunning awe taking a look at what showed up to be a Goddess of the finest rearing and excellence. Wearing what must be the most striking shading accumulation, short sleeved shirt with sleeves impending mid-route down her arms and short shorts with each shading flawlessly adjusted like an interwoven of the most extreme detail; a magnum opus of extent in a collection of magnificence enhancing her delightful, physically formed body and each form highlighting her sound firm build. Ms. Ok Eun Suk was perched on a turquoise hued throne laying on an oval formed stage of just a couple of centimeters thick enhanced with substantial white padded arm rests and a high back that finished in a point simply over her head. Minsu remarked to Jimin saying that she looked the American Wonder Woman individual he saw playing volleyball as they drew nearer the Turquoise Palace; the particular case that was winning all the volleyball coordinates all alone. Jimin remarked, "Ms Ok Eun Suk is better dressed and significantly more shocking with more balance and a more extensive arrangement of shading than simply red, white and blue and it doesn't appear to be likely that such a lady would be playing volleyball outside the Turquoise Palace. Go ahead Minsu; what are you considering? How would she be able to be playing volleyball one day and afterward be hoisted to such a magnificent, dependable position as female authority of the Turquoise Palace of Korea Past and Present the following day? It is more likely than not to have been another person. I think you're having a ton of fun Minsu" Indeed, every shading possible, past the seven shades of the range were perfectly balanced and could be seen with white and turquoise adorned in more clear detail, particularly beneath her belly. On her legs from her feet up to simply over her knees she wore white and turquoise patent calfskin skin tight boots; white from the toe to just underneath the knee and after that turquoise "sleeves" right over the knee closure in a point with both hues consummately supplementing each other. If at any point there was a paragon of human magnificence that had ever lived, a lady that was head and shoulders or light years above whatever else then Minsu and Jimin were seeing her in all her quality. Gradually, she turned her head to look to where Minsu and Jimin were standing: Nam Jae Young was simply behind and somewhat off to one side like a pleased guardian remaining with his kids and after that his consideration moved back to the focal point of consideration, gazing up in astonishment and marvel, transfixed by the minute at what was in front of him. Ms. Ok Eun Suk connected with her open hand upward to get the sword. Minsu immediately uprooted the sword from his side and held it by the handle in one hand with Jimin remaining to one side holding his other hand. Minsu, being the immaculate noble man, held the sword up and introduced it to Ms. Ok Eun Suk; this was most likely the best snippet of his life and one that he would delight in for quite a long time to come. The expression on his face, as he gave the sword to her demonstrated a young man at the most elevated point or peak of his minute in time: genuine right now at time of presentation with a "trailing" grin after the exchange like a student being given a recompense for commendable results in a troublesome school examination or making the last goal that got his group the trophy for winning an association football game or Taekwondo competition. Both kids could feel the force and excellence of this lady as she took a look at them. As she took the sword she mysteriously suspended it over their heads and gradually moved it toward her whereupon she took it and put it in a sheath around her side. At the point when the procedure was finished she gave them a wonderful, warm and charming grin, looked straight ahead, from where she sat and afterward leaned back in her throne. Gradually her vehicle started to rise; straight up it went as the kids observed in surprise and stood amazed at how she could do that. They were both as yet gleaming from her grin and vicinity until she vanished into the highest point of the palace, gone until they proved unable to see her any longer. Each of the three were all the while gazing up long after she vanished attempting to see where she went, stricken and charmed. The greater part of the movement that had solidified in position continued: feathered creatures were singing and the hints of creatures and water from the adjacent creek carried on as though continuous. Both kids were still shining long after she "touched" them with her appeal, power and warmth. "Wow that was justified regardless of the entire voyage, just to see that!" Minsu shouted like a tyke who had quite recently been given a Playboy magazine. The experience gave them both another feeling and fortified their course and pride as Koreans and adoration for Korea. "How about we observe the Sunshine Policy of President Kim Dae Jung. We ought to see a pioneer who truly endeavored to unite our partitioned nation. He truly tried and attempted to bring more noteworthy political contact in the middle of North and South from 1998 to 2007." As the youngsters entered Kim Dae Jung's module they were stricken by how youthful he looked and how unmistakably he communicated his thoughts. Minsu and Jimin unmistakably saw that the purpose behind the strategy was to unwind the North's mentality towards the South by building closer monetary ties and relations. Kim was thought to have been conceived on 6 January 1924, yet it is accounted for that he later changed this to 3 December 1925 to keep away from enrollment amid the time when Korea was under Japanese provincial rule. . "Kim Dae Jung" Kim was conceived in Sinan in what was then the Jeolla region; the city is presently in Jeollanam-do. Kim moved on from Mokpo Commercial High School in 1943 at the highest point of the class. In the wake of filling in as an agent for a Japanese-claimed sending organization amid the Japanese control of Korea, he turned into its proprietor and turned out to be exceptionally rich. Kim got away from the Communist catch amid the Korean War. "Kim Dae Jung". Encyclopædia Britannica. 2009. In 1992, Kim made yet another fizzled offer for the administration, this time singularly against Kim Young-sam, who had consolidated the RDP with the decision Democratic Justice Party to frame the Democratic Liberal Party (which inevitably turned into the Grand National Party). Many thought Kim Dae-jung's political vocation was adequately over when he took a rest from legislative issues and left for the United Kingdom to take a position at Clare Hall, Cambridge University as a meeting scholar. "Board of Advisors – Kim Dae-jung" However, in 1995 he reported his arrival to governmental issues and started his fourth journey for the administration. The circumstance got to be ideal for him when general society rebelled against the occupant government in the wake of the country's monetary breakdown in the Asian money related emergency weeks before the presidential race. Partnered with Kim Jong-pil, he vanquished Lee Hoi-chang, Kim Young-sam's assigned successor, as the decision hung on 18 December 1997. When he was confirmed as the eighth President of South Korea on 25 February 1998, it denoted the time in Korean history that the decision party calmly exchanged power to an equitably chosen restriction victor.["Kim Dae Jung". Encyclopædia Britannica. 2009 "Opposition boycott shadows South Korea's new president" The race was damaged with discussion, as two hopefuls from the decision gathering split the progressive vote (38.7% and 19.2%

separately), empowering Kim to win with just 40.3% of the prevalent vote. "1997 South Korean Presidential Election" Kim's boss adversary, Lee Hoi-chang, was a previous Supreme Court Justice and had graduated at the highest point of his class from Seoul National University School of Law. Lee was generally seen as an elitist and his application was further harmed by charges that his children evaded required military registration. Kim's instruction conversely was constrained to professional secondary school, and numerous Koreans sympathized with the various hardships that Kim had endured already. Kim Dae-jung took office amidst the monetary emergency that hit South Korea in the last year of Kim Young-sam's term. He enthusiastically pushed financial change and rebuilding suggested by the International Monetary Fund, in the process altogether adjusting the scene of South Korean economy.After the economy shrank by 5.8 percent in 1998, it grew 10.2 percent in 1999. in actuality, his arrangements were to make for a more pleasant business sector by holding the intense chaebol (aggregates) responsible, e.g., more prominent straightforwardness in bookkeeping practices. State endowments to expansive organizations were significantly cut or dropped. The two Korean summit gatherings in Pyongyang of June 2000 and October 2007 were the first of their kind and attempted to work out a few distinctions. "Kim Dae-jung: Dedicated to reconciliation" He found himself able to win a seat in the House in the resulting races in 1963 and 1967 and went ahead to turn into a prominent resistance pioneer. All things considered, he was the regular resistance possibility for the nation's presidential decision in 1971. Kim was verging on being murdered in August 1973, when he was captured from an inn in Tokyo by KCIA specialists because of his feedback of President Park's Yushin program, (Yushin Constitution adopted in October 1972 and confirmed in a referendum on 21 November 1972) which conceded close tyrannical forces. A long time later, Kim considered these occasions amid his 2000 Nobel Peace Prize address. "He was likewise honored the Noble Peace Prize for this so I think we ought to discover his module" Minsu said in a cheering way. Under Kim Dae Jung's organization the Sunshine Policy was initially defined and actualized. The national security strategy had three fundamental standards: No equipped incitement by the North will be endured; The South won't endeavor to retain the North in any capacity; the south effectively looks for participation. There were likewise two other significant approach segments: the division of legislative issues and financial aspects which fundamentally implied that the South would extricate limitations on its private area to make interests in North Korea to enhance the North's economy and to instigate change in the North's financial strategy. The second part was the necessity of correspondence from the North so that every administration would regard one another as equivalent every making concessions and bargains. Two months into the Sunshine Policy when the South asked for the creation of a get-together habitat for separated families in return for manure help the North impugned it as a type of "horse trading". The rationale of the approach was in light of the perfect that in spite of the hardships the North perseveres through, the North's administration won't fall. At the point when President Roh Moo-hyun proceeded with the approach of his forerunner relations really enhanced from 2002 however, in 2003 the issue of the North's ownership of Nuclear weapons surfaced and the U.S. blamed both sides for rupturing the structure. "It would appear that we just about had peace there for a period." said Jimin who went ahead to say, "yet it appears to be neither side could truly believe the alternate's goals." Despite the fact that the approach was announced a disappointment by the South Korean Unification Ministry it was the nearest the two sides have ever come to assertion since the war finished." Kim died on 18 August 2009 at 13:43 KST, at Severance Hospital of Yonsei University in Seoul. "Former S. Korean President Kim Dae-Jung Dies" The reason for death was given as various organ brokenness syndrome. An interfaith state burial service was held for him on 23 August 2009 before the National Assembly Building, with a parade prompting the Seoul National Cemetery where he was entombed by customs. He is the second individual in South Korean history to be given a state memorial service after Park Chung-hee. He kicked the bucket around 3 months after the ninth South Korean President Roh Moo-hyun conferred suicide on May 23, 2009. The Wikileaks information uncovers that the U.S. International safe haven in Seoul depicted Kim as "South Korea's first left-wing president" to the American government on his day of death. Barbara Demick (19 August 2009). After leaving the module both kids reflected on the disappointments of different frameworks of government and wondered about how Korea has continued through history to unite at different times and also, turn into a country that ought not be isolated. "There will be one Korea once more," praised Minsu. "Take a look at the disappointments of Russian socialism." included Jimin. Minsu identifies with Jimin similarly an instructor converses with an understudy or guardian to a kid and said, "How senseless it is for a gathering of individuals to be separated over something as feeble and transient as legislative issues. We are one glad country united by our antiquated legacy and the way that we all talk one dialect and essentially originate from the same source. That is the quality we would have in one glad country. Why do we let absurd men choose the fate of our Korea? Why do we let such contrasts interfere with us? All individuals ought to be free and everyone has the privilege to appreciate a glad and prosperous life; not to be mistreated and made to endure an existence ailing in solace and bliss. Korea has battled against outside and inner strengths for a huge number of years and won't stop until it is under one administration that ought to be for the individuals; by the individuals and the greater part of the people. After that devoted, awakening background." Jimin felt there was more to investigate on the same topic. Entering the module Minsu and Jimin had the capacity to see where Syngman Rhee was conceived in Hwangae Region "Syngman Rhee". Reference book Britannica on April 18 1875 in North Korea. 이승만 [李承晩 [Rhee Syngman]. The kids were astounded at how some individual could have originated from such a modest, unobtrusive starting and ascend to turn into the first president of South Korea and how he was so centered around his battles for a free and united Korea, practically from the beginning. "His experience ought to be a motivation for everyone who may think they don't originate from the correct place or have the right begin in life; a few individuals need to begin right from the base. It's the determination to ascend that constructs character and quality." expressed Minsu with the demeanor of a guardian or theory educator. The entire time in the Turquoise Palace saw development of the kids well past their peers. Jimin, on occasion, thought she could recognize Minsu's voice experiencing the change. Having the capacity to follow his heredity the distance back to Lord Taejong of Joseon Cha, Marn J. (September 19, 2012) and a sixteenth era relative of Amazing Ruler Yangnyeong, Rhee's family moved to Seoul when he was just 2 years of age. 이승만 [Rhee Syngman]. Reference book of Korean society (in Korean). In Seoul he got the customary Confucianism preparing and was a conceivable possibility to enter the Korean common administration as a contender for gwageo, the common administration examination. However in 1894 changes annulled the gwageo framework so he enlisted in the Pai Chai, an American Methodist School and after that in 1895 he functioned as the principle author for the two daily papers Hyeopseong Digger and Maeil Shinmoon. y 이승만 [Rhee Syngman]. Reference book of Korean society (in Korean). Breen, Michael (April 18, 2010). Right now Rhee changed over to Christianity while at school and afterward inevitably moved on from Pai-Chai school 이승만 [李承晩] [Rhee Syngman]. Doopedia (in Korean) and there he taught Americans Korean. Breen, Michael (April 18, 2010). Rhee changed over to Taoism 이승만 [李承晩 [Rhee Syngman] in the wake of being arraigned in a plot to take revenge for the death of Ruler Myeongseong. Luckily, he was excused from this charge when a female American doctor bailed him out. He went about as the author sorting out dissents against the negative impact of Russia and Japan in Korea. Breen, Michael (April 18, 2010). Rhee was sent to Kyung Moo Cheong jail in January 1899 이승만 [Rhee Syngman] as far as it matters for him in a plot to evacuate Lord Gojong with the assistance of Park Yeong-hyo. In 1904, Rhee was discharged from jail at the flare-up of the Russo-Japanese War through the assistance of Min yeong-hwan and in November 1904 he moved to the United States. 이승만 [李承晩] [Rhee Syngman] In August 1905 Rhee and Yun Byeonggu met with Secretary of State John Hay and U.S. President Theodore Roosevelt in New Hampshire where he attempted to persuade the U.S. to help Korea protect its autonomy Yu (유), YungEek (영익) (1996) yet this exertion was not effective 이승만 [李承晩] [Rhee Syngman] While in a state of banishment in the U.S. he got a B.A. from George Washington College in 1907; a M.A. from Harvard Uninversity in 1908; 이승만 [李承晩] [Rhee Syngman] Cha, Marn J. (September 19, 2012) [1996], and a Phd from Princeton College where he composed a proposal on impartiality. "Syngman Rhee: First president of South Korea". Syngman Rhee. On August 1910 he came back to Japanese Korea where he worked at the YMCA as a facilitator and preacher. 이승만 [Rhee

Syngman] In the wake of being involved in the 105 man occurrence and in the end captured which was one of a few endeavors by for the most part Korean Christians to kill Masatake Terauchi, who was the Representative General of Korea. In 1912, 105 were sentenced to hard work detainment and only 6 had their sentences forced yet then they were discharged in 1915. In 1912 Rhee fled back to the U.S. where he attempted without accomplishment to get the then president Woodrow Wilson to help those sentenced in the 105 man occurrence. In December 1918 Rhee was picked as one of Korea's agents to the Paris Peace Gathering and afterward in 1919 by the Korean National Affiliation yet did not pick up consent to go to Paris. 이승만 [Rhee Syngman]. Being not able to go to Paris, Rhee held "The First Korean Congress" in Philadelphia with Seo Jae-pil to set up a system for the revelation and autonomy of Korea. 이승만 [Rhee Syngman] When the disturbance of the Walk first Development settled, Rhee was advanced and discovered himself designated to the positions of Remote pastor in NoRyoung Temporary Government and Leader for the Temporary Legislature of the Republic of Korea in Shanghai and a position equivalent to president for the Hansung Temporary Government. (Syngman Rhee: First president of South Korea" "Syngman Rhee") The Cool War Records. From December 1920 to May 1921 he moved to Shanghai and satisfied his position as acting president for the Temporary Government. 이승만 [Rhee Syngman]. Mitigated of his obligation as the president of the Temporary Government in Shanghai over charges of abuse of force and was expelled from his occupation. (Breen, Michael (November 2, 2011). Notwithstanding the setback he proceeded with he kept up his autonomy exercises through the Korean Commission to America and Europe. He took an interest in the Alliance of Countries gathering in Geneva, in mid 1933, to mix up a few considerations and feelings for Korean autonomy.

y 이승만 [Rhee Syngman]. In November 1939 Rhee and his wife left for Hawaii and in the mid year of 1941 he concentrated on his book, "<u>Japan Inside Out</u>," which was truly a push to caution the U.S. and England of Japan's aims. With the Japanese assault on Pearl Harbor he utilized his position as the administrator of the outside relations division of the temporary legislature of Chungking; his aim was to pick up acknowledgment of the Korean temporary government by President Roosevelt and the U.S. State Office. y 이승만 [Rhee Syngman]. After the surrender of Japan and Korea's freshly discovered freedom on September 02 1945, Rhee had a stealthy meeting with General Douglas MacArthur whereby Rhee came back to Korea in 1945 on McArthur's plane, the Bataan. Cummings, Bruce (2010). After coming back to Korea he turned into the president of the Autonomy Advancement Focal Council and president of the Headquarter for Unification and the Individuals' Illustrative Popularity based governing body. 이승만 [Rhee Syngman. He was contrary to the Moscow gathering which proposed isolating Korea into 4 territories and questioned any collaboration between the socialist and national gatherings. He was continually pushing for Korea to be perceived as a free substance. 이승만 [Rhee Syngman). On July 20 1948, Rhee was chosen president of the Republic of Korea with 92.3% of the vote; the second applicant Kim Gu got 6.7%. Croissant, Aurel (2002). On August 15, Korea as a Republic was formally settled. Not long in the wake of taking office Rhee made laws that entirely diminished any political difference utilizing a more unbending type of government and numerous radicals were captured. Amid the Korean war both Rhee and Kim wanted to unite Korea with their own particular style of government. Toward the beginning of threats in 1950 all South Korean resistance at the 38th parallel was immediately squashed and stifled. At the point when Seoul was possessed by

North Koreans, Rhee set up an interim government in Busan. The Rhee government was extremely degenerate from the President on down and everybody was taking the cash and help from the United States. It has been expressed that amid the war Rhee's pay was $37.50 every month. (Merrill, John). The Rhee government occupied with the "more regrettable overabundances of defilement" (Hastings, Max The Korean War) possible. Hastings composed that the Rhee administration occupied with the "more terrible abundances of debasement" with the warriors in the ROK Army going unpaid for quite a long time as their officers stole their pay, the hardware gave by the United States was sold on the underground market and the span of the ROK Army was bloated by countless "apparition troopers" that just existed on paper to permit their officers to take the pay that would had due these fighters on the off chance that they had really existed. The issues with low resolve experienced by the ROK Army were to a great extent because of the defilement of the Rhee regime. The more regrettable embarrassment amid the war, to be sure of the whole Rhee government was the National Defense Corps Incident outrage. (Hastings, Max *The Korean War*, New York: Simon & Schuster, 1988 page 239) Because of wide zones of debasement and political suppression Rhee endeavored to change and revise the constitution so he could hold elections for the presidency by mainstream vote. The gathering didn't oblige this thought so Rhee had the majority of the political resistance captured . He then passed the coveted revision and in July and in the accompanying presidential decision he got 74% of the vote. Buzo, Adrian (2007). At 84 years of age Rhee won another term (his fourth) as President with 90% of the vote after his adversary (Cho Byeong-alright) died. At the point when Rhee was testing Chang Myon and won the vote by a wide edge, allegations of vote apparatus began to rise which maddened areas of the Korean public openly. Lee surrendered when a few demonstrators were shot in endless supply of the Blue House. Rhee kicked the bucket of a stroke in Hawaii on July 19, 1965 and after one week his body was flown back to Seoul where he is covered in the Seoul National Cemetery. ("Syngman Rhee" The Cold War Records) "Wow, he beyond any doubt had a fascinating life and what battles he had as well, yet it all paid off for him, notwithstanding being ousted he guided and formed Korea into what it is today." lauded Jimin. "We have such a great amount to be appreciative for, as Koreans." included Minsu . Soon after leaving the module Nam Jae Young approached where the kids were standing and admired the highest point of the arch and then afterward looked down at them and said, "She's gone and now it's your time to go back. Just join the amulets together and say, we miss Sacheon." The children could detect a sense of sadness and grief in his voice as he knew he would never see them again. "Thank you, Mr. Nam Jae Young for all your help and guidance" Jimin said looking up at him with the almost same feelings of grief and sadness that she felt the morning she woke up and found Oonky stiff and motionless; it was time to say good bye to a good friend. "Just before we go we would like to find Kim Yushin's module now that Nam Jae Hoon's sword has been returned. We just want to see how he helped to unify Korea and how he kept it under the kingdom of Silla for more than 200 years." With that little request and fond farewells (Jimin gave him a little kiss on his cheek when he bent over to hug them) and tears abound both youngsters cleared a path and in the long run discovered the module of the relentless seventh century warrior General Kim Yushin conceived in 595 in Gyeyang, Jincheon province. He was the child of General Gim Seohyeon and Woman Manmyeong; an individual from the illustrious group of Gaya, a relative of the last ruler of Gaya and was the immense grandchild of Lord Guhae of Geumgwan Gaya; Ruler Guhae saw the end of the Geumgwan (Gaya) state. In what is referred to in antiquated Korea as the "bone rank framework" or golpum (arrangement of noble rank that was utilized as a part of Silla and was utilized to isolate the layers of society on the premise of innate and closeness to the throne and the power they were allowed to wield.) McBride, Richard D., II. General Kim Yu-sin had a high bone rank framework which permitted him to do practically do whatever he needed to do. At just 15 years of age he was an expert swordsman and Gukseon or Hwarang pioneer by the age of 18. The Hwarang, otherwise called the "Bloom Young men" of the Silla kingdom were a tip top gathering of guys with mutual basic hobbies for expressions of the human experience and society which had its sources in Buddhism. His youth name was Sandara and he is very viewed as maybe being the best general and soldier in Korean history. He was the primary power for the unification of the Korean promontory under Rulers Muyeol and Munmu of Silla and is viewed as the best broad in the unification wars of the kingdoms period. Kim Yusin's sister wedded his nearby companion and kindred spirit Lord Ch'un Ch'u which fortified the bond between them. In 611 amid the rule of Lord Chinp'yong when Gim was just 17 years of age Goguryeo and Baekje were beginning to attack Silla region. The chafed Kim Yusin withdrew to a mountain, fasted and promised to put an end to the issue. Following 4 days an old man came to Gim and said, "Despite the fact that you are youthful, you are of decided nature to bring together these three kingdoms (Silla, Baekje, Goguryeo), this absolutely shows an in number character. After the old man taught him his mystery he vanished in a splendid light of five hues. (Il-yeon: Samguk Yusa) Legends and History of the Three Kingdoms of Antiquated Korea. A lot of what is thought about his life is found in the Samguk Sagi: a recorded history of the Korean kingdom. As Silla was in a consistent battle with its neighboring kingdoms of Baekje and Goguryeo over domain, General Kim was continually demonstrating his aptitudes and achievements as a skilled General; his first engagement happened in 629 at 34 years old when he was raised to the rank of 7 star General and the authority of Silla. Battling under his dad, Sohyun when his troops lost the will to battle after fizzled endeavors to take vanquish Nangbi Mansion Gim Yusin battled his way into the adversary camp and decapitated one of the officers. In the wake of seeing this his troops encouraged on to battle and decapitated 5,000 a greater amount of the adversary troops. Chu, Yo-sŏp. 1947. Kim Yusin of Silla united with the T'ang Line in an exceptionally uneasy organization together against its adversaries. (McBride, Richard D) Amid the Clash of Hwangsanbeol with the help from the Silla naval force and 130,000 T'ang powers the kids had the capacity perceive how the General chop down his adversaries on the front line and assaulted Baekje and Goguryeo powers at the Baekje capital of Sabi. Under the order of General Gyebaek the Baaekje powers of around 5,000 men were no match for Gim's warriors. Chu, Yo-sŏp. 1947. Kim Yusin After Bakje Gim and his T'ang associates in 661 proceeded onward to overcome the verging on invulnerable Goguryeo kingdom however were repulsed. Goguryeo was debilitated by this assault and in the end devastated in 668 after another hostile was propelled in 667. The General needed to quell a few pockets of resistance yet he needed to verify that the T'ang Chinese didn't exceed their welcome and in 668 Promotion the General was all around remunerated for his endeavors: Ruler Munmu regarded him with the privileged title of Taedaegakgan which means Preeminent Messenger of Barrier practically lifting him to the rank of Executive. Nahm, Andrew C. 1983. Gim Yusin lived to be 79 years of age in 673 and is the center of various stories and legends. The kids had the capacity see where was covered and saw that he was granted with another privileged title; that of Heungmu. McBride, Richard D., II Despite the fact that he never saw the last result of his consistency and battles, he got under way the predetermination for Korea's pleased history and the kids delighted in the entire time they watched him from their vantage point inside the immense General's module and life. Through his whole life the General felt that Baekje, Goguryeo and Silla ought not be discrete but rather united in one kingdom. He is viewed by numerous as the main thrust in the unification of the Korean landmass and is the most acclaimed general of the considerable number of commanders in the unification wars of the Three Kingdom Period. "Before we go I might want to take one final look at another kingdom and the last Line of Korea: the Joseon Administration which was the last kingdom to administer Korea. Since we are here we ought to benefit as much as possible from our time as we won't have the capacity to ever do this again." beseeched Jimin in a spur of the moment last claim; other than that history is enjoyable. Both youngsters had a certain aversion about leaving their ideal enterprise; they never acknowledged the amount of fun live history could be and were appreciating the experience of Korea as it happened. When they entered the module they were both cleared away by the quality, difference and extent of achievements by this kingdom. Both kids had the capacity to witness the distinctive systems for standard amid the Joseon (1392-1910) period despite the fact that it was authoritatively renamed the Korean Realm in October 1897. 조선". 한국민족문화대백과. After death lifted to the rank of Head by Gojong who had announced the Korean Domain in 1897, Taejo of Joseon (October 27, 1335-June 18, 1408) conceived Yi Seong-gye whose name is Yi Dan can make the case of being the first ruler of the Joseon Tradition and its organizer and who was likewise the primary individual who ousted the Goryeo

Administration. Lee, Jun-gyu. The family name or last name of the line was Yi. Byonghyon, Choi (2014). The Archives of Lord T'aejo: Organizer of Korea's Chosŏn Line. Cambridge, Mama: Harvard College Press. Yi Seong-gye was a general in the Goryeo armed force and was known as a gallant pioneer. He ascended through the positions and grabbed the throne in 1392. He set up the Joseon Administration and named after the old Kingdom of Gojoseon. (Gojoseon at Doosan Reference book) After the ruler signed up with Jeong Do Jeon they brought a capable group bringing the quality of the military and artistic together. Yeon Do Jeong was the rule modeler of the Joseon administration setting set up the ideological, institutional and legitimate structure. Taejo delegated him to the most noteworthy regular citizen and military office entrusting him with all the important energy to set up the new administration. Lee, Yeong-hee (4 February 2014) His profound thought insightfulness (Jeong Do Jeon) began influencing Korean legislative issues. (Seoul district site). The sovereigns were contending with themselves as well as with the new government priests. Jeong Do-jeon trusted that the administration pastors and not the ruler ought to decide. (Lee, Yeong-hee (4 February 2014). The decay of Buddhims in the last a large portion of his guideline was a because of debasement and the ascent of solid against Buddhist logic and assumption. Kim, Djun Kil (Might 30, 2014). Jeong Do-jeon was against Buddhism and in the long run supplanted it with Confucianism. (Han Yeong-u. (1974). In 1394 the capital was built up at Hanseong (Seoul). (Seoul district site). Issues emerged when he picked a child to succeed him in 1398 in what came to be known as the First Strife of Sovereigns which was that year he abandoned. Startled at how his children were willing to kill one another over the throne and as yet grieving the demise of his second wife he instantly delegated his second child Yi Blast gwa as lord who later got to be Top dog Jeongjong . Yi Blast won, Taejo's fifth child was likely the best decision to succeed the throne as he contributed the most to his dad's prosperity however he harbored a significant contempt of against two of his dad's key associates: the Executive JeongDo-jeon and Nam Eun. (Lee, Jun-gyu) In 1400 Ruler Jeongjong contributed his sibling Yi Blast won as beneficiary in the wake of Lord Jeongjong relinquished the throne. Yi Blast won accepted the throne as Ruler Taejong in 1400. Taejo passed on in 1408 in Changdeok Royal residence. Regardless of his prosperity at usurping the throne and freeing himself of the authorities who stayed faithful to the old administration he was seen by numerous as a progressive and definitive ruler who nullified the old, maladroit, outdated framework and cleared a path for the new. He permitted Korea to revamp and rediscover its way of life. The longest governing ruler was Yeongjo who ruled for a long time (1724-1776) as the 21st lord. Ruler Yeongjo held his Confucian standards profoundly. "The historical backdrop of Korea". Archive.org. His rule was checked by persevering endeavors to change the assessment arrangement of Joseon run by Confucian morals and diminish and accommodate the factional infighting under his "Brilliant Amicability" Strategy. His administration has been called a standout amongst the most splendid rules of the Joseon Line. "The historical backdrop of Korea". Archive.org. He was dependably in a steady condition of stress and sympathy toward his kin and how to enhance the worker's life. One day Yeongjo woke up to the sound of downpour and was stressed over a surge and how it would destroy the harvest and reason his tragic individuals to starve. He was anxious to teach his kin by disseminating books in Korean script. (The Archives of Yeongjo dated July 27 of the fourth year of his rule 1728). There were 27 rulers of the Joseon Administration who all ruled with diverse abilities and shortcomings and who were the majority of the

Jeonju Yi group and slipped from Taejo. Under Confucian rationality the ruler summoned outright power from authorities and subjects. Through this Confucian rationality some of them conveyed a feeling of relentlessness to the nation while others didn't do extremely well by any stretch of the imagination. There were nine rulers in a little more than 100 years which implied there was a great deal of progress; the initial three resigned. The main lords of the Administration were extreme, solid, battling men who favored nature to whatever else. Amid the Joseon Tradition a letters in order was made; improvements in climate anticipating were picked up and upgrades in war innovation helped them to safeguard themselves from outside assaults and permitted the Koreans to keep up their freedom for a considerable length of time. The main hopeless occasion amid his time on the throne was the passing of his Sovereign Sado. Ruler Sado experienced maladjustment haphazardly murdering individuals in the castle and was additionally a serial attacker. Since the lord couldn't kill his own child he with the assent of Woman Yi who issued a regal pronouncement that he ought to move into a rice midsection where passed on 8 days after the fact. The Diaries of Woman Hyegyeong. Lord Injong was the most limited term ruling ruler which went on for one year from 1544-55. Talk has it that he was harmed so his stepbrother could take the throne. Ruler Sejong of the Joseon tradition, truly combined his tenet over the Korean landmass and saw an awesome time for advances in common science, farming, building and writing and is thought by numerous to be the most productive; he is stand out to two to get the sobriquet of "Incredible". Sejong was conceived on May 15, 1397 as the third child of Lord Taejong (Reference book of World History, Vol II, P362) and at 12 years old he got to be Stupendous Sovereign Choong Nyung. Conceived as the third child in the middle of Taejong and Ruler Partner Min and after his more seasoned sibling was stripped of the title Great Sovereign, Sejong climbed to the throne.. Picked over by his two sibling by demonstrating extraordinary capacity in his studies his rising to the throne was truly one of a kind by the way he circumvented his two more established siblings. Taejong's eldest child Yangnyeong was the following in line to succeed as beneficiary obvious but since of his inclination for relaxation exercises and recreation exercises Taejong picked Sejong. After being made lord, Taejong's second child turned into a friar. (Reference book of World History, Vol II) In 1418, Taejong relinquished for his child Sejong yet even in retirement Taejong kept on affecting control. It wasn't until Taejong's demise that Sejong's political brightness got to be apparent. Reference book of World History, Vol II, P362 Sejong. After being Above all else, Sejong changed everything by advancing and designating individuals from distinctive social positions to end up common workers. Keeping up the solid Confucian impact he urged individuals to act with the Confucian standards and in light of this Confucianism turned into the socially acknowledged method for doing things. The Lord likewise distributed a few books about Confucianism. At first the Lord attempted to stifle Buddhism yet then he acknowledged it by making a test to turn into a Buddhist minister or Seung-wa. The ruler proceeded onward a wide scope of approaches keeping up great relations with Japan and permitting exchange with them. To stifle the irritating privateer circumstance he attacked Tsushima island with military powers . (Reference book of World History, Vol II, P362) Sejong with respect to the Ming circumstance he made a few strategies that profited Joseon. The ruler likewise saw the need to reinforce the military and he ended up being a compelling military organizer. Y⌐ng-gyu, Pak (2004). He shaped different military strategies to reinforce the protection of his country. Varieties sorts of mortars were tried and in addition fire bolts to attempt and overhaul the innovation of his munitions stockpile. In May 1419, Ruler Sejong with the assistance of his dad had chosen to put an end to the Japanese privateer circumstance out of Tsushima Island. As an after effect of this exertion 245 Japanese were executed and 110 were taken as detainees of war. They additionally served to free 150 Chinese seize casualties and 8 Koreans. 책 한권으로 읽는 세종대왕실록. What the lord was truly keen on doing was Science and Innovation. He delighted in the domain of innovations and changes and energized the advancement of moveable metal sort which was initially utilized as a part of Korea in 1234. He additionally made changes to sturdier mulberry paper which improved quality books for all Koreans. He had the first rain gage created, sundials and extremely exact water timekeepers; maps of stars and heavenly globes. Ranchers, he thought required a handbook so he chose to make an agriculturist's handbook which would help with the planting and reaping of products. 책한권으로 읽는 세종대왕실록. The book called the Nongsa jikseol was similar to a reference book for escalated development procedure. "Since we have seen the perspective from South Korea how about we observe how North Korea turned into the way it is with its socialist type of government and since we are here." expressed Minsu. "I realize that his arrangements may appear to be frightful and repulsive to anyone from South Korea but I think we ought to see the opposite side of the "page" and why North Korea is the way it is." argued Minsu. His module just about mirrors Kim Dae-Jung's in area so we should go inside. Without a doubt enough his module was right opposite where they were standing. Both kids were hesitant at first to go in as they dreaded they may not have the capacity to get out... Once inside the youngsters noticed how the "environment" appeared to be so much colder and genuine. There wasn't anywhere to sit and the survey range was restricted in its degree and separation of perspective. Both kids were altered to the range that demonstrated Kim Il Sung's life right from the earliest starting point. A starting sound transcript placc everything in context for the kids. Credited with being the first comrade ruler utilizing the decisive word" "Juche" (Herman, Steve (13 July 2004)) which was his term to depict confidence and patriotism in another Korean framework, at no other time seen on the Korean peninsula; Juche in the long run supplanted Marxism-Leninism and socialism as something particularly Korean in nature. Paul French (2014). North Korea: Condition of Neurosis. Zed Books) Kim Il-Sung was conceived Kim Sung Chu however received the new name Kim Il-Sung in 1935 which means "day of the sun" after a renowned Korean guerilla pioneer who battled against the Japanese amid their control of Korea. Kim Il-Sung held more than one office before turning into the preeminent pioneer of the Democratic People's Republic of Korea (DPRK) in 1948 and the first comrade head of state to build up dynastic tenet. Baik Bong (1973) Conceived on the fifteenth of April 1912 (after death known as "Day of the Sun") in Man'gyondae, Pyong-namdo territory, Korea (North Korea) to workers. (Soviet Officer Uncovers Insider facts of Mangyongdae) Both of his guardians were effectively occupied with the religious group; his maternal granddad was a Protestant pastor and his dad had gone to an evangelist school and was a senior in the Presbyterian church. "Subside HITCHENS" Byrnes, Sholto (7 May 2010) At 7 years old his dad Kim Hyong jik moved the family to eastern Manchuria to get away from the Japanese who were controlling Korea at the time. "Take a look at how how opposed he was to utilizing the Japanese dialect by scratching out, with a penknife, the Japanese titles of his textbooks since he wanted to communicate in Korean." said Jimin. Subsequent to going to the center school in Kirin, he joined the Socialist party of China in 1931; the Comrade gathering of Korea had been established in 1925 and had been rejected for being excessively nationalistic in the 1930s. Kim asserted to have won-more than 100,000 engagements with the Japanese somewhere between 1932 and 1945 which implies Kim would have needed to win no less than 20 for every day, constant over a 13 year period. Kim in the long run fled to the Soviet Union close to the start of World War 2 to the Soviet Gathering school of Khabarovsk. Jasper Becker (1 May 2005) After the war a ton of conceivable suitors went to Seoul and appearing for authority employments planning to oversee the nation. Right now the nation was partitioned into North and South Korea by the Russians and Americans at the 38th parallel. Kim situated himself with the Soviet-adjusted communists and in the wake of incapacitating his adversaries set him up as head of the Law based Individuals' Republic of Korea when it was established in 1948. Regardless of United Nations arrangements to lead all-Korean races, the Democratic People's Republic of Korea was announced on 9 September 1948, with Kim as the Soviet-assigned head. In May 1948, the south had pronounced statehood as the Republic of Korea. On 12 October, the Soviet Union perceived Kim's administration as sovereign of the whole landmass, including the south. DPRK Foreign Relations

By 1949, Kim and the Communists had merged totalitarian tenet in North Korea and all gatherings and mass associations were either dispensed with or united into the Democratic Front for the Reunification of the Fatherland, a well known front however one in which the Workers Party prevailed. Around this time, the "clique of identity" was advanced by the Communists, the first statues of Kim showed up, and he started calling himself "Incredible Leader" Jasper Becker (1 May 2005) The three unmistakable communists were the Soviet adjusted who had quite recently come back from the Soviet Union; the Chinese adjusted who had recently come back from China and the local gathering who were against the Japanese vicinity in Korea. Hoare, James E. (2012) From 1948 till 1994 Kim solidly settled himself as the one in force and one of his first goes about as Head was to persuade the Soviets that he could without much of a stretch move over the 38th parallel to overcome the South in three weeks which he in the end did on June 25, 1950. Stalin helped Kim thus did Mao Tse-tung however it all arrived at an end on July 27, 1953. Concentrating now on disposing of the Soviets by the mid 1960s and to free himself of every one of his foes. Kim's standard got to be in view of trepidation, obliviousness and disengagement from whatever is left of the world. Baik Bong (1973) Kim was unequivocally keen on a tenet of nationalistic independence known as Juche: Kim is the expert of the Korean people groups' predetermination. With his accentuation on enhancing agribusiness creation and industry from 1953-1970 things really did function admirably for Kim; at one point the North was in preferable monetary condition over the South. It was likewise more than simply political talk; North Korea added to the most autarkic (independent) economies on the planet. Despite the fact that North Korea got a considerable measure of help and help from comrade China and the Soviet Union, it didn't join Comecon, the socialist basic business. Then again, with military spending coming to one-quarter of the whole spending plan and decay of harvests and his trucks no more drawing in the Soviet interest things started to get ugly and the economy started to crumple. Just to some thought of how vain Kim was, for his sixtieth birthday he had an immense bronze statue raised. 김일성, 쿠바의 "혁명영웅" 체게바라를 만난 날. DailyNK . On July 08, 1994 Kim passed on of a heart attack which sent North Korea into a condition of grieving and discouragement. Gradually Minsu and Jimin, subsequent to sitting on the floor for what felt like a day, both got up and left the module. They were both feeling somewhat dismal and pain for their North Korean neighbors. "I can't comprehend his state of mind and I don't perceive how anyone could profit by his method for administration. Does that sound like a kind and altruistic ruler?" mourned Jimin. "Could you envision King Sejong treating his kin like that? The premise of King Sejong's guideline was his adoration and sensitivity for the normal individuals. This clown administered on the premise of apprehension, fear and obliviousness for the customary individuals." said Minsu. "That was not an exceptionally cheerful affair perceiving how Kim Il-sung treats his kin and anyone who didn't concur with him was killed" included Minsu. "The fellow was only a tormenting, unstable, dictator " Beyond any doubt it sounds like a fizzled framework to me, particularly when they're prevented fundamental rights from claiming flexibility and the quest for satisfaction. What a shaky failure" expressed Jimin. After exiting the Turquoise Palace and standing just outside the entrance for one last look both children stood together and prepared for their out of time departure. "Hold my hand Jimin and give me your half of the amulet." Minsu said. Jimin reached into her pocket pulled out the amulet half and held it up against Minsu's half. "Say with me, 'we miss Sacheon'." In the flash of a light both children were back. "Wow, we're back at Jinju castle, Minsu. That was great!" Jimin exclaimed with thrill and excitement at how suddenly and quickly it had all happened. They were back at the exact same location in the same time just as they had left; a light rain shower had just started so they stayed under the cover of the castle for a few minutes until it ended. "Things sure look different now than they did back then, don't they? I am so glad to be back here in more familiar times." said Minsu. Glancing down the road Minsu could see their bus coming. "Quickly Jimin, I think I can see bus number 111." Both children climbed out from under the shelter and ran up the large white stone boulders, across the road and anxiously awaited the arrival of the bus. "Wow, it sure feels weird to be waiting for the bus!" exclaimed Jimin. Both children raced to get on the bus and found an empty seat in the back and sat down both very happy to be back in more familiar surroundings. "The first thing I am going to do when I get back to Sacheon is have a milkshake at Lotte burger and some fries." said Minsu with Jimin eager to take him up on his request. As the bus made the short trip from Jinju both children were ablaze with so much to tell from the experience of their journey; to have seen Korean history as it happened was something that nobody, from any time would have ever experienced. Nam Jae Hoon had gone and now the children were anxious to see if their new found mental powers, as Nam Jae Hoon had promised, were really going to help them at school. They had already seen some of it before they left. Looking out the window of the bus at the cars, trees, buildings, and people Minsu couldn't stop thinking about Ms. OK Eun Suk and her radiant beauty, that gorgeous smile and her magnetic charm. How did she move Nam Jae Hoon's sword without any physical support? All of this and their whole trip had to be put down to fantasy and a lot of mystery. More than anything he wished he could have had one of those devices she was able to travel on; how did it move so silently and smoothly without any noticeable signs of thrust? After getting off the bus at the Sacheon bus terminal and walking the short distance between the parked cars and buses to the Lotte hamburger restaurant, Minsu and Jimin felt like they could talk of just about anything in Korean history now. After finishing their meal both children were anxious to get home and see their mom and dad and jump into their fresh, warm, soft, clean beds. Not having to worry about whether they had to flee or hide for their lives from any big soldiers riding big horses or eat any horrible food was a big relief. The whole episode had an enormous maturing effect on the children enriching them in mental years well beyond their contemporaries; they were now young adults having endured some very adult situations. It had been an exciting journey and one that they would never, ever forget.

Printed in the United States
By Bookmasters